Dodge City

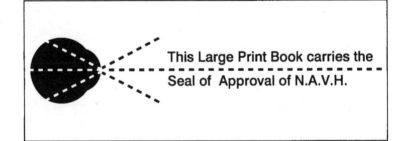

DODGE CITY

Barry Cord

WHEELER PUBLISHING

Published in 2004 by arrangement with
Golden West Literary Agency.

Wheeler Large Print Western.

The text of this Large Print edition is unabridged.
Other aspects of the book may vary from the original edition.

Set in 16 pt. Plantin by Minnie B. Raven.

Printed in the United States on permanent paper.

Library of Congress Cataloging-in-Publication Data

Cord, Barry, 1913–
    Dodge City / Barry Cord.
      p. cm.
    ISBN 1-58724-602-3 (lg. print : sc : alk. paper)
    1. Dodge City (Kan.) — Fiction.   2. Large type books.
I. Title.
PS3505.O6646D63 2004
   813'.54—dc22   2003070533

DODGE CITY

As the Founder/CEO of NAVH, the only national health agency solely devoted to those who, although not totally blind, have an eye disease which could lead to serious visual impairment, I am pleased to recognize Thorndike Press★ as one of the leading publishers in the large print field.

Founded in 1954 in San Francisco to prepare large print textbooks for partially seeing children, NAVH became the pioneer and standard setting agency in the preparation of large type.

Today, those publishers who meet our standards carry the prestigious "Seal of Approval" indicating high quality large print. We are delighted that Thorndike Press is one of the publishers whose titles meet these standards. We are also pleased to recognize the significant contribution Thorndike Press is making in this important and growing field.

Lorraine H. Marchi, L.H.D.
Founder/CEO
NAVH

★ Thorndike Press encompasses the following imprints: Thorndike, Wheeler, Walker and Large Print Press.

1

The trooper from Fort Union was drunk, bored, and mean. He hated civilians, hated Santa Fe, and he had just been rolled by one of the red-light girls north of the Plaza. This was his first liberty since coming off extended patrol, and he was at odds with the world and looking for trouble.

He spotted it just ahead of him.

The tall, well-dressed man was coming out of the Wells Fargo office, still reading a telegram he held in his hand. To the trooper the man was obviously a well-heeled civilian, which only added fuel to his thirty-dollars a month anger.

He lurched forward, jammed his shoulder into the tall man, and snarled: "Get the hell outta my way!"

Luke Ryatt held him off, saying mildly: "Sure, soldier." He had other things on his mind, and he didn't want trouble with the military. Not in Santa Fe.

He started to walk around the angry trooper, shoving the telegram inside his pocket. But the soldier from Fort Union wasn't about to let Ryatt off that easy.

"Goddam civilians!" he swore, "think you own the town."

He lunged forward, driving a fist at Ryatt's face. Ryatt ducked, frowning. It looked like he couldn't avoid it. He jammed the heel of his right hand under the burly trooper's chin as the man came at him again, flailing away with both hands. The man's head snapped back, and he staggered, cursing wildly.

Ryatt flicked a glance at the trooper's companion, an older, mustached man wearing a lance corporal's stripes. He wasn't as drunk as the burly soldier, and he didn't want this kind of trouble.

He tried to stop it. "For Chrissakes, Sully —"

Sully shoved him away and started to reach for his holstered Army pistol. Ryatt didn't want to kill him. He stepped up close and kneed him in the groin. Sully gasped, doubled, both hands clutching his middle. His eyes showed a lot of white, his sun weathered features paled.

Ryatt spun him around, marched him to the horse trough on the edge of the plank-walk, and jammed his head into the scummy water. The trooper's hat came loose and floated away.

The lance corporal started to go for Ryatt, but stopped as Ryatt's right hand snapped up, a snub-nosed derringer appearing in it.

He said angrily: "Goddammit, mister — you're drowning him!"

Ryatt grinned coldly. "Might be what he deserves." He jerked the burly man's head out of the dirty water, spun him around, and shoved him toward his companion.

Sully staggered, coughing up water. . . . He fell to his hands and knees and started to shake himself like a dog coming out of a pond.

The corporal bent over him and started to help him up. "Jeesus, Sully," he muttered. "If we git picked up —"

He stiffened and looked back into the Plaza as a military contingent clattered into view . . . he stepped away from Sully, shoulders squaring with a soldier's instinctive reaction to the presence of an officer.

Lieutenant Smalley, supply officer, swung sharply in toward the walk and pulled up a few yards away. The supply wagon, flanked by two uniformed troopers, halted in the middle of the Plaza.

Sully was on his feet now, swaying a little, his eyes still clouded. The lieutenant ran his cold gaze over him, lips tightening. He turned his attention to Sully's companion, frowning.

"Someone giving you trouble, trooper?"

The corporal bit his lip and eyed Ryatt. "No," he muttered. "Jest a little misunderstanding, Lieutenant. Sully was drunk . . ."

"No harm done," Ryatt said.

Lieutenant Smalley eased back in his saddle and turned his cold gaze on Ryatt. The lieutenant was a young man, newly commissioned. He took his rank seriously.

"I'll be the judge of that!" he snapped.

Ryatt shrugged.

"You new in town?"

It was none of the lieutenant's business. Ryatt just stared at him, his cold gray eyes telling him to go to hell.

Anger rocked the lieutenant forward, his hand sliding down to his Army pistol. Then he spotted the derringer in Ryatt's fist, down by his side, and he thought better of it.

"Manhandling troopers is a military offense, mister!" he snapped. "Just remember that!"

He turned back to the lance corporal. "Get Sully back to the fort!" Anger still crackled in his voice. "I'll make sure he sleeps it off in the stockade!"

He gave Ryatt one last, long look before pulling his mount around and riding stiffly across the Plaza, the men behind him following.

Ryatt released his grip on the derringer, and it slipped back into a sleeve holster. It was a trick he had picked up from a Mississippi riverboat gambler.

The older trooper was having his hands full with Sully, who plainly was no longer interested in trouble.

10

"Goddammit, Sully," the corporal snarled, "let's get back before that squirt lieutenant throws the book at us!"

Neither he nor Sully gave Ryatt a look as the tall man walked past them, then cut across Santa Fe's central plaza, passing by a stone monument with a plaque that read: *"To the Heroes Who have Fallen in the Various Battles with Savage Indians in the Territory of New Mexico."*

Ryatt paused to light a slim cigarillo. Behind the Plaza, seemingly no more than a stone's throw away, loomed the Sangre de Cristo Mountains, snow-capped most of the year.

Ryatt liked Santa Fe. The air was clear, and even in midsummer it never got too hot. It nestled on a seven thousand foot plateau, at the foot of the Sangre de Cristos, and the Pueblo Indians called it the Land of the Dancing Sun.

It had been an Indian town first, and then Spanish . . . the two cultures had blended in homes fashioned after the ancient pueblos at Tesuque and Cochiti and in Spanish colonial buildings on the Paseo de Peralta.

The American fort just outside of town intruded a jarring, if necessary note into the easy pace of Santa Fe life. With the troopers had come the red-light girls, Spanish *putas* and big Norwegian girls, settling in houses and cribs along the old Santa Fe trail.

Ryatt shrugged. Like a lot of things, Santa Fe was changing.

The Peralta Hotel was at the south end of the Plaza. The lobby was empty as Ryatt stepped inside, crossed to the desk, and paused to reread his telegram. It was from an old friend:

Town needs help. $15,000 sound right? Come quick.

It was signed *Ned Coster*, and it was sent from Dodge City.

Ryatt slipped the telegram into his pocket and looked around. Thick adobe walls shut out the growing morning heat and outside noise. A large oil painting of General Peralta hung on the wall by the carpeted stairs. The brick red floor tiles were worn smooth by long use. Leather-backed chairs stood stiffly against the window wall, facing a long, low oak table.

The hotel had an air of old Spanish elegance, which suited Luke Ryatt just fine. It was quiet, peaceful, and the service was excellent. A stock of imported wines and champagne cooled in the wine cellar.

The Hotel Peralta was one of the several places Ryatt came to, after a job. He always had the best room in the house reserved.

He hated to leave it. But his hobbies were expensive, and his money was running low. He shrugged. Fifteen thousand dollars sounded just about right.

12

And he figured the trouble in Dodge City must be an emergency, or Ned Coster would not have wired.

The desk clerk was not around. Ryatt went behind the desk and slipped money into his numbered pigeonhole. He had done this before. Jose would understand.

He went quickly upstairs, opened the door to a large room fronting on the Plaza, crossed quietly to the heavy oak bureau, and pulled out a drawer.

The woman in bed stirred, sighed softly, and said: "Luke?" in a dreamy, voluptuous voice.

Ryatt went to the wardrobe and took out a Boston bag. It was already packed for traveling; in it were his work clothes and the tools of his trade.

He carried it back to the bureau, took off his coat, and unhooked his sleeve holster. He shoved the holster into the Boston bag and tucked the derringer in his waistband. From the bureau drawer he took out a pair of matched Colts, bonehandled and oiled. He checked them carefully, then started to buckle the black leather cartridge belts around his lean waist.

The woman came awake now, propping herself up on one elbow. She was nude, the covers falling away from a full, rounded breast as she watched Luke.

"Where are you going?" Her voice was still sleepy.

Luke shrugged. "Out."

He could see her in the mirror, a mass of golden hair falling past her white shoulders as she sat up in bed. She was pouting. Her name was Belinda. She had the looks and mannerisms of a Southern belle, but beneath the velvet softness was steel. She had told Luke she had been born on a South Carolina plantation, that her family had been wiped out in the war. It was probably a lie, but Luke never questioned a woman in matters like that. She was not old, but she had been around . . .

"It's barely daylight," she said. Her voice held a careful rebuke.

"Eleven o'clock," he corrected her.

She eyed the Boston bag at his feet. "You're leaving Santa Fe?"

He nodded. "Business."

His eyes were steel gray, hard. They could look through a man, cold and appraising. He was a tall man, wide through the shoulders, lean-hipped. He had a rider's toughness, his sense of distance. He would be thirty-one next October; he had been born on a West Texas ranch run pretty much as a Southern plantation by his Virginia-born father and mother. They had tried their best to develop in Luke a taste for the finer things of life — he still retained a love of women, champagne, and fast horses.

Luke went into the Civil War fighting for

the Confederacy, but he emerged from it nonpolitical. Death, he found out, was a great leveler. He went back home to find his parents dead, the ranch gone. He was faced with earning a living, but jobs were scarcer than hen's teeth in Texas and returning veterans not particularly welcomed elsewhere.

Still, the war had taught Luke Ryatt how to survive, and how to use guns. He had become as adept with a howitzer as with a Colt .44.

And in the wild booming frontier towns that were springing up west of the Mississippi, Luke found a ready market for his talents.

Belinda slid a long, shapely leg out from under the covers, dangling it. She asked softly: "Business? Where?"

Ryatt finished tying his holster down and turned. "Dodge City." He grinned. "Want to come along?"

"Dodge?" She shuddered and settled back, disappointed. She had momentarily entertained hopes of going with Luke. But Dodge . . . *Christ, not Dodge!*

"How long?"

"Can't say."

In a corner of the big bedroom, over by the window, a caged mynah bird, black as Hades and twice as sinful, hopped up to its perch and screamed: "How long, Luke?"

Luke dug a cracker from the glass cookie jar on the dresser and dropped it into the cage. The bird tried to nip a chunk from Luke's fingers, missed, and cursed like a trooper. He jumped down from his perch to the floor of the cage and cocked a suspicious eye at the cracker before taking a quick peck at it.

Luke said casually: "Keep an eye on her, Jethro."

The mynah bird looked at Belinda, cocked his head to one side, and blinked one eye. "Okay, Jake." He took another peck at the cracker. "Okay, George."

Luke frowned. The little, black-feathered bastard must be in cahoots with her.

He turned to Belinda. "George, eh? Jake?"

The girl eased back on her pillow, a breast still exposed, a dark nipple erect, beguiling.

"A lady has to live," she murmured.

He grinned. No arguing that. He picked up his bag. "The room's paid until the end of the month. I could be back before then."

She slid her bare leg suggestively back and forth along the side of the bed. "That's a long time, Luke." Her eyes were dark violet . . . soft, teasing. "One for the road?"

Luke thought it over. What the hell, business could wait. Thirty minutes longer, anyway.

He put the bag down and started to take off his pants.

2

Luke Ryatt took the stage out of Santa Fe. It was six years before the railroad would reach here; a horse would have taken him longer, and Ned Coster's telegram had sounded urgent.

The old Butterfield stagecoach rocked along on its leather springs. A trained Indian fighter rode shotgun. The five passengers kept their arms ready.

It was roughly three hundred and fifty miles to Dodge, most of it through Indian country. Only a few months earlier there had been a massacre at Adobe Walls; a band of Comanches had cornered a bunch of grubby buffalo hunters and all but wiped them out. The scare had flashed up and down the old Santa Fe trail. Stagecoach passengers took turns spelling the shotgun guard, the rest keeping their rifles oiled and ready.

The stage crossed the Pecos River at Pajarito and swung north past Fort Union and Wagon Mound. Just beyond, the road split, the northern branch climbing up into the Rockies, topping at Raton Pass and dropping down to Bent's Fort on the upper Arkansas. This route was usually snowed in nine months of the year, but in summer it was the least dangerous (from Indian attack) and cooler. But it was the long way around to Dodge, and Butterfield passengers out of Santa Fe usually had a choice.

The older branch of the Santa Fe swung northeast out of Wagon Mound, crossing the Little Canadian and heading into the dreaded Desert Route, which had been called earlier by the Spaniards the *Jornada del Muerte,* the Trail of Death.

Armed men stood guard at the stage relay stations. The passengers saw small bands of buffalo hunters following herds down the Cimarron and heard the boom of the big Sharps buffalo guns. Once they were held up by the crossing of a buffalo herd, moving north to escape the fierce summer heat. They saw no Indians.

They rested a half day at the Upper Springs Station while men worked changing one of the leather braces and regreasing the big wheel hubs.

Heat and dust were a problem; water was scarce and doled out sparingly. No one complained.

They rolled in to Dodge eight days later. They came in at noon with the heat rising up from the slow moving river, blanketing the sprawling town on the bluffs. It was the fifth straight day of vicious Kansas plains heat, and the end was not yet in sight.

The stage thudded across the plank bridge and slanted down Front Street running parallel to the Santa Fe rails. Dust rose and hung in the turgid air behind the coach, powdering the ugly frame buildings. What breeze there was brought the acrid smell of cattle crowding the stock pens just outside of town. Their bawling made a continuous undertone.

The stage slewed to a stop in the Plaza. It was too early in the day for the shills, the bunco men and gamblers, the harpies and the whores to be about, and the heat was keeping most of the others indoors. The Plaza showed a couple of wagons tied up before Rath's mercantile store, a hipshot saddle horse in front of a hole-in-the-wall saloon.

A sour-faced man in shirtsleeves, sweat rings showing under his armpits, came to the door of the stage office and watched as the leathery-faced driver unloaded baggage.

"See any Indians?"

It was a stock question. Luke had heard it asked by every relay station agent along the Cimarron route.

The driver ignored it. So did the cold-eyed shotgun guard who brushed past the agent, heading up the street with his rifle and warbag tucked under his arm. He had survived his run and had a few days rest coming before he took the run back.

The four passengers who had ridden out of Santa Fe with Ryatt were tired, thirsty, grimy, and in no mood for idle chatter. They picked up their baggage and hurried off, two of them crossing to the Santa Fe railroad station to buy tickets to Kansas City.

Ryatt lingered, slanting his gaze across the sun-beaten dusty Plaza. The last time he had been here it had been a buffalo hunter's town, a squalid collection of tents and shacks on the empty Kansas prairie. Vast buffalo herds roamed just below the river. Skinners and long-shanked buffalo men came here to toss away a year's earnings on skull-popping whiskey and wild women, with horny-handed railroad graders and mule-skinners giving them competition. But even then it had boasted of more saloons, gamblers, and whores to the square foot than could be found in any other town, east or west of the Mississippi.

It was bigger now, and wilder, according to the stories coming down the trails. With the arrival of the railroad in the fall of '72 had come the Texas longhorns, streaming up the old Chisum Trail to Abilene, slanting off along the way, just below the Canadian, and blazing a new trail to Dodge that became known as the Western Trail. And with them had come the bunco artists, the grifters, gunmen, and more whores to prey on Texas

20

drovers with trail pay in their pockets and hell in their eyes.

Ned Coster hadn't said what the trouble was, but it usually fell into a pattern. Someone had the town treed, and the city fathers needed help. Gun help.

Ryatt picked up his bag. The town was beginning to stir. A man came to the door of the Long Branch Saloon and dumped a bucketful of dirty water into the street. Further on a woman stuck her head out of an upstairs window and surveyed the Plaza, then withdrew it. A dog came out of an alley, shied away from the hot sunlight, and lay down in the scant shade of a water barrel, tongue lolling.

The driver was going into the office. Ryatt heard his exasperated voice crackle: "Goddammit, Henry, I said no Injuns! What were you expecting, another massacre? Just be happy it was a quiet trip!"

Quiet enough, Ryatt thought. But the way the hunters were wiping out the buffalo herds meant trouble. Already small mounds of bleached buffalo bones dotted the rolling prairie south of Dodge. Hell, the Cheyennes and the Kiowas would take only so much . . .

He headed for the Dodge House. On the way Ryatt passed two hole-in-the-wall saloons, a greasy spoon restaurant, and a bawdy house. Only the restaurant showed some sign of life.

The desk clerk was a pale-faced man with a wispy blonde mustache. He was sorting mail into pigeonholes, and he eyed Luke with little regard. Gamblers were a dime a dozen in Dodge, and Luke, dressed in black pants and long black coat, looked like one to him.

He watched Luke sign the register, the name meaning nothing to him. With the coming of the railroad, notables from all over the world, the rich and the important, riding in elegantly-appointed sleeping cars had come to visit Dodge, "the wickedest city west of the Mississippi." They went on safaris with experienced buffalo hunters, sporting expensive silver-mounted, high-powered rifles to bag a few shaggy bison heads as trophies.

There was a note of snobbery in his tone as he said: "Bath's down the hall. But you'll have to wait your turn."

Ryatt shrugged. The bath could wait. He asked where he could find Ned Coster.

The clerk had turned around again, sorting through the mail. He said discourteously: "Really, sir, I have no idea where —"

Ryatt was tired, dirty, and impatient. He reached across the desk, jerked the clerk around.

"*Where?*"

The clerk's Adam's apple bobbed. "Sorry." He glanced again at the register. "Mr. Ryatt, you'll have to ask Mr. Coster's widow."

Widow?

Christ! Luke hadn't even known Ned Coster was married. Hadn't been, the last time he'd heard from him.

"Where do I find her?"

"O'Hara's Lodgings, down the street. Turn left on North." The clerk pulled back as Ryatt loosened his grip. He smoothed his shirt front, his tone going sullen: "If she's still there."

Ryatt put money on the counter. "Have someone take my bag to my room. I'll be back shortly."

He needed a shave, and a change of clothes. A bath would have helped. But if Ned was dead, it could change things considerably. He didn't like coming all the way from Santa Fe for nothing.

The sun blasted down at him from a cloudless sky as he stepped out of the Dodge House. But in the north, at the far edge of the plains, thunderheads were piling up. If the wind picked up there could be a change by nightfall.

Ryatt crossed the Plaza, stepped aside as a pair of hard-eyed men, armed and insolent, rode across his path. They were wearing trail-faded clothes, Confederate forage caps. They gave him a casual look as they continued on, heading for the area south of the deadline.

South on Front Street, just before the North Street intersection, the town fathers had erected a large board sign that said plainly:

WEARING OF FIREARMS BEYOND
THIS POINT IS PROHIBITED.
By order of:
The Town Marshal.

The sign was shot full of bullet holes. One of the two riders drew his holster gun and added a couple more as they rode by.

O'Hara's Lodgings turned out to be a narrow-fronted, two-story building wedged in between a tack shop and a Chinese merchant specializing in powdered buffalo horn as a "restorer of manhood."

Ryatt walked up to the fan-lighted front door, knocked, waited a few moments, then stepped inside, the afternoon heat wearing at his patience and civility. He went down the hallway, glanced inside the front parlor, saw no one there, and continued on toward the back of the house where a staircase led to upstairs bedrooms.

The woman in the kitchen doorway had her back to Luke, listening with evident distaste to what was going on upstairs.

Ryatt looked her over. Ned Coster would have been crowding fifty by now, although he would never have admitted it. A raunchy rooster of a man, he had been Ryatt's platoon sergeant during the war.

He said "Mrs. Coster . . . ?" and had to repeat it, louder, before the woman noticed

24

him. She was short and stout, all of fifty, gray-haired, wise, and unabashed by men.

"Mrs. Coster? Hah!" She pointed upstairs. "That's her . . ."

A string of unladylike curses floated down-stairs. Ryatt shrugged and headed for the stairs. The woman barred his way.

"And who may you be?" she demanded.

"A friend of the family."

He pushed past her, the wooden steps creaking under his weight. A narrow hallway greeted him at the end of the stairs. He paused, locating the voice before moving, past peeling wallpaper, toward an open door midway down the hallway.

A black man was kneeling on the lid of a small, hide-covered trunk in the middle of the bedroom. He was sweating profusely, oily drops sliding down his face.

A woman was standing by him, her back to Ryatt. She was dressed for travelling, a furled parasol in her right hand. She used it to tap the black man sharply on his bared head.

"Goddammit, Johnson, if I miss the stage I'll have your black hide —"

Ryatt intruded. "Mrs. Coster?"

She turned. Ryatt had expected an older woman. This one couldn't be a day over twenty. Fair-skinned, rich brown hair, stacked to the hilt. A pheasant feather jutted from the brim of the small hat on her head.

Amber eyes rifled him. Full lips curled distastefully. Ryatt looked like some scroungy, down-at-the-heels tinhorn looking for a handout.

"Who in hell are you?"

"Ryatt," Luke said coldly. "Luke Ryatt."

"Oh!" Surprise shaped her mouth. "Oh, my God!" She surveyed him more carefully now.

"Jesus Christ!" she said angrily. "You're late!"

"I came as soon as I received Ned's wire."

The hostility slipped from her face. She smiled, sighed heavily. It could be an act — she was the type.

"Yeah — I'm sorry. I guess I should have wired you." She brushed a tear from her eye. "Ned's gone, Luke . . ."

"Dead?"

She nodded. "A kindly old man . . . a real gentleman . . ." She sniffed, pulled out a lace handkerchief from her sleeve, and held it to her face. "The only man I ever loved . . ."

Ryatt choked on this one.

The black man had managed to clamp the lid down on the trunk. He stood up now, waiting.

"When did he die?"

"Three days ago," the woman said. She sank down on the bed, as though the recollection was too painful. "They found Ned hanging from the barn beam at the Corby farm. Committed suicide, they said . . ."

"Old Ned?" Ryatt scowled. "Why?"

She shrugged. "That's what they said." She eyed him covertly, appraising him.

"Who're they, Mrs. Coster?"

"Christ, call me Sadie!" she said sharply. She stood up and snapped at the black man. "What in hell are you waiting for, Johnson? Get your ass down to the stage station with that trunk!"

She turned to face Ryatt.

"You coming?"

Ryatt shook his head. "I just got here."

The black man hoisted the trunk to his shoulder. Sadie gave him a silver dollar as he went out.

"You're a fool if you stay," she said. "Ned's dead. You came too late."

She rummaged through her carpetbag, came up with a bottle, and looked at him.

"You like Scotch?"

"I'd rather champagne," Ryatt said.

She eyed him. "It's Scotch or nothing."

Ryatt shrugged. "No use wasting it." He could stand a couple of stiff drinks.

Sadie found two glasses on the stand by the washbowl. She filled them, killing the bottle.

Ryatt raised his glass. "Well, here's to your late husband, Ned Coster . . ."

"He was a goddam fool," Sadie said. "But I'll drink to that."

They drank. Ryatt was surprised to find it was pretty good Scotch.

He said: "I didn't know Ned was married."

"Happened five days ago," Sadie said. "Won me in a crap game over at the Lady Gay." She didn't elaborate.

It sounded like Ned Coster, Ryatt thought. Crazy like a fox. Ned had lost an arm at the battle of Caleb's Mill, and for a while it looked like he was going to die. The Army surgeon pulled him through, but Ned figured he was living on borrowed time from then on and decided he'd make the most of what years were left.

Sadie slugged her drink down and coughed. "I'm getting out of Dodge while I can," she said. "Before the Colonel gets a wild hair up his ass and comes looking for me. . . ." She smoothed her skirt down around rounded hips and slanted a look at Ryatt.

"I know Ned sent for you. He told me he would. He was hoping you'd get here be-fore . . ." She hesitated, eyes narrowing, voice going softly bitter. "They killed him, Luke. Even if they made it look like Ned committed suicide. There's nothing more you can do here now —"

Not for Ned, maybe, Ryatt thought grimly. But he had come here on the promise of a job. He couldn't do it alone. He had to have had the approval of the city fathers —

"Where can I find the Mayor?"

"Kelly?" Sadie made a wry face. "Spends a lot of time out of town. But if he's in Dodge, he's either playing poker at the Long Branch, or sleeping one off at his house behind the church."

Ryatt finished his drink.

"You still staying?"

Ryatt's grin was cold. "If the price is right." He put his empty glass down on the dresser.

"Have a good trip, Sadie."

He left her staring after him as he went out.

3

"Fifteen thousand dollars," Ryatt said flatly. "That's my price, gentlemen!"

The meeting was being held in the Mayor's house. Luke had found him in the Long Branch Saloon; the Mayor had rounded up the rest of the city councilmen — four men who, with Kelly, more or less ran Dodge City.

Ryatt was standing by the piano in the Mayor's front room. It gleamed with high polish; it was seldom used. A framed tintype atop it pictured a younger looking Kelly with a prim-faced woman and two small children.

The others were scattered around the room. Kelly lounged in a horsehair-stuffed chair, a spittoon by his side. He was a cigar smoker, a pink-faced man in his fifties, bald, a fringe of white hair, hard blue eyes. Shrewd eyes. He owned stock in the railroad, had interests in the buffalo-hide trade, and was president of the Dodge City National Bank. His wife hated Dodge City and wouldn't live here. Kelly spent part of the time with her in Hays City, most of the time here. He liked the arrangement.

Kelly leaned forward, used the spittoon, and eyed the others. He was in shirtsleeves, his collar unbuttoned. All the windows were open, but it was still hot in the room. Smoke made a blue haze against the ceiling.

"If you can clean this town up," he said bluntly, "it's worth it. If you can't —"

"You don't owe me," Ryatt cut in. His cold gaze raked the others in the room. "Fair enough?"

Lorry Gray, a short, stocky, watery-eyed storeowner, pursed his thin lips: "It's a hell of a lot of money, John." Besides the store, Gray ran a freighting business and owned warehouses. "A hell of a lot of money to pay for a lawman . . ."

"How much are you losing in trade?" the Mayor snapped back. "All of you? A thousand a month? More?"

Lorry sighed. "Too much," he admitted. — "But —"

"I'll go for it," Morry Teague growled. He was a big man, both physically and in influence. He was the western representative and manager of feed lots for a big Chicago meat-packing firm, and he bought most of the Texas beef coming up the trail to Dodge.

He shifted his legs, crossing them as he eyed Ryatt. "I say it's cheap at the price, if he can do it."

Angus MacIntosh, Scotch born, forty, tough as whalebone, said flatly: "He won't last the weekend. Sure, I know Ryatt's reputation. Still," he said, putting on his pipe, "one man . . . ?" He shook his head. "Need an Army here, that's what!"

Ryatt picked up his hat. "Get the Army then," he said shortly.

He turned to leave. "Good day, gentlemen!"

"Wait!" Kelly swung around to face the Scotsman. "Goddammit, Angus, you know the soldiers up at Fort Dodge have their hands full with the Indians. And ever since that Army nigger corporal was killed in town they've been told to keep their troopers out of Dodge. What we have here is civil trouble. That's what the Governor calls it. That means we handle it, not the Army!"

Angus puffed unconcernedly on his pipe. "We hired a couple of town marshals before," he pointed out. "The first one was run out of town. The other one was killed —"

"Gentlemen!" Ryatt cut in coldly. "I'm not interested in what's happened. Ned Coster wired me the town needed help. He said the situation was urgent. And the price he quoted was fifteen thousand dollars —"

"Who in hell authorized Coster to send that wire?" Gray demanded.

"I did!" Kelly snapped. "He came to me right after that last marshal we hired was shot and said he knew a man who could do the job for us."

He looked angrily around at the others. "You all know the situation here. The town's wide open. We got riffraff coming in from all over. We've got a law office standing empty. There's shootings all over town. We need a lawman, and we need one fast!" He turned to Ryatt. "Far as I'm concerned, you're hired!"

Morry Teague shrugged.

Angus MacIntosh puffed on his pipe. "I'll go along with it."

Lorry Gray chewed on the edge of his sorrel mustache. "Damn high price for a town marshal," he muttered.

Kelly ignored him, turning his attention to the one man who up to now had not said anything.

"How about you, Fred? You in?"

Fred Gelson nodded. "Makes sense to me." He was a small, wiry man, with gray-shot hair standing like a stiff brush on his head. Ink-stained fingers. Eyes a faded blue, cynical, tired from long hours of proofreading under oil lamps. He was the owner and publisher of the *Dodge City Weekly Gazette*.

Kelly eased back in his chair.

"That's settled then." He turned to Ryatt. "What will you need?"

"A badge, the keys to your jail, and your assurance you'll back me all the way." He eyed the others, a small smile on his lips. "All the way, gentlemen."

Fred Gelson frowned. "Now wait a minute," he said mildly. "That's asking a lot —"

"I've got my own ways of doing things," Ryatt cut in flatly. "I'll probably be stepping on some toes." He ran his gaze over the men in the room. "I don't want to have to argue with a committee about every move I make."

Fred looked undecided. Lorry Gray chewed on his mustache. "I don't know —"

Kelly overrode him. "Just keep it legal, Ryatt, and we'll back you."

Ryatt nodded. "Fine. Now, where's the trouble. Who's behind it?"

"It's centered south of the deadline," the mayor answered. "Bars are wide open. Full of toughs, drifters, gunmen, yahoos. They used to confine their killings to that end of town. Now —"

"For Christ's sakes, John — tell him the truth!" Angus snapped. "The Colonel's the big trouble here, and everyone in this room knows it!"

Ryatt frowned. "The Colonel?"

Kelly looked embarrassed. "Texas cattleman by the name of Morgan. His men call him the Colonel. Wears a Confederate officer's tunic. He came up the trail a couple of weeks ago, trailing a thousand head . . ." He looked at Morry Teague. "You bought his herd, didn't you?"

"You know damn well I did!" Morry

snapped. "That's my business, buying Texas beef. And he was paid a fair price for his steers." Morry's voice, despite its growl, sounded defensive. "Can I help it if the market for Texas beef was down?"

"Eight dollars a head," Fred said blandly. "Way down, wasn't it, Morry?"

Morry glared at him. "Goddammit, whose side are you on, Fred?"

Lorry Gray muttered: "I thought we were here to hire a town marshal —"

Kelly held up a pacifying hand. "Cut it out, Fred. Morry made the Colonel a legitimate business deal. The man took Morry's money, didn't he?"

"What choice did he have?" Fred muttered.

Morry stirred, eyes hardening. "Are you saying I — ?"

"Shut up, Fred!" Kelly ordered. "You, too, Morry! Fighting among ourselves isn't going to get us anywhere!"

He turned to Ryatt. "Angus is right. The Colonel is the big problem here. He and his trail hands have taken over the Lady Gay. They've stopped all other Texas herds coming up the trail to Dodge. Most of them are swinging back to Abilene. The last marshal we had was shot when he went after the Colonel in the Lady Gay."

Kelly paused, reached for his whiskey glass, and took a long swallow.

"Might as well know what you're getting

into," he muttered. "The Colonel's given this town an ultimatum. Morry comes up with the difference, or he and his men will come across the deadline —"

"Twenty dollars a head!" Morry sneered. "The bastard's crazy! There wasn't enough tallow on his steers when I bought them to make a half dozen good candles!"

He stood up and swung his big bulk around to Ryatt. "I've got quotas to fill, beef to ship back East. I want you to get that goddam fool out of my hair! That's what I'll be paying you for! Run him out of town, or kill him! I don't give a damn which, just get him out of my hair!"

Ryatt shrugged.

Morry picked up his hat. "Now if you'll excuse me, gentlemen," he said stiffly, "I've got some business to attend to."

The others watched him leave in silence.

Angus put his pipe away. A breeze stirred the limp curtains framing the windows. Somewhere in the distance thunder rumbled.

Angus got to his feet. "Guess I'll mosey on home before that storm hits . . ."

He looked at Ryatt and smiled faintly. "You've got a job cut out for you. Good luck, Marshal."

Lorry Gray fiddled with his mustache. He had gone along with the others, but he didn't like it.

"Guess I'll head on back to the store," he

muttered. "Not that there's much business these days . . ." He glanced at Fred. "You coming?"

Gelson stood up. "We need the rain." He looked at Ryatt. "I don't give you the chance of a snowball in hell," he said. His tone was mild, a faint smile in his blue, cynical eyes. "But, keep what you do legal, and I'll back you all the way."

Kelly waited until they were gone. "I guess I have to agree with Fred," he muttered. "I wouldn't give a rat's ass for your chances. But Ned said you were good . . ."

He stood up and dropped his soggy cigar butt into the cuspidor.

"Come on. I'll show you to your office and swear you in."

4

The Dodge City law office faced the Santa Fe depot, north of the deadline. A newly built, red brick building, it had two barred windows facing the street and two cells in back. A rabbit warren of tarpaper shacks sprawled out behind it.

A work train was moving out of the yard, heading west as Ryatt and the Mayor paused in front of the building. The Atchinson, Topeka & Santa Fe was building beyond Dodge, reaching for Denver. Most of the railroad crews, the gandy dancers and railroad graders, were camped fifty miles west, making only occasional forays now into town.

Kelly took a key ring from his pocket, fitted a key to the padlock, and opened it. They went inside just as lightning flared, the jolt of thunder rumbling.

Ryatt looked around the office as Kelly went to the desk, pulled out a drawer, and came up with a badge. He handed it to Ryatt and swore him in. Ryatt put the badge in his pocket.

The rumble of thunder sounded closer. A

breeze blew into the room. It had the smell of rain in it.

Kelly smiled. "Ain't had a decent rain in more than a month. Maybe it's a good omen." He looked around the office. "Anything else you need?"

Ryatt shrugged. He was standing by the window, looking out. It was late afternoon and the clouds had caught up with Dodge. The town looked gray, drab, waiting for the storm to hit.

"I'll be staying at the Dodge House," he said. "Any objections?"

Kelly shook his head. "Charge your room to the city," he said. "Your meals, too. Don't mind standing for your liquor, either. Just keep the tab reasonable."

Ryatt smiled faintly.

Kelly turned to go. Ryatt said: "What happened to Ned Coster?"

Kelly took a long moment before answering. "He hung himself."

Ryatt frowned. "Why?"

"I don't know," Kelly said. "I didn't know him too well. Kind of a loner, Ned was. Only friend he had was Jeff Corby —"

Ryatt came away from the window. "Corby?"

Kelly nodded. "They were old friends. About a week ago Jeff got himself killed. Left a wife, two small kids." The mayor shook his head. "Jeff was a quiet sort of man. Never could figure out why he went to the Lady Gay that night . . ."

He looked at Ryatt. "You knew Corby?"

Ryatt nodded. "Same outfit in the war. 'C' Company, Third Battalion, Texas Volunteers . . ." He turned back to the window, his voice thinning. He had not expected this.

"Jeff Corby, Ned Coster, and I served under a Captain by the name of Wayne Morgan . . ."

Kelly was surprised. "You think . . . the Colonel . . ."

Ryatt's voice was grim. "Could be. I heard he went back home, started putting a ranch together . . ."

Kelly frowned. "Well, this sort of changes things, doesn't it?"

"Why?" Ryatt asked bluntly. "Why should it?"

Kelly hesitated. "The war's over. I've never asked a man's politics, or what side he fought on —"

"Don't!" Ryatt said coldly.

"He was your C.O. —"

"He was a hard-nosed bastard," Ryatt said. "If he's the same man. Did everything by the book. But he never hung behind in a fight . . . and he treated his men fair."

"You still want the job?"

Ryatt considered. "The war's over, Kelly," he said quietly. "Times change. Men, too. If it's the same man, and he's breaking the law . . ."

Kelly eyed him for a long moment, making up his mind. "Your keys to the office are in the desk. A man comes in once a week to clean up. Name's Olaf, a Swede. Serves as jailer, if you need him. Good man."

He went to the door, looked up at the lowering sky. "Yeah," he said casually, "it's going to rain."

He looked back at Ryatt, shaping his words. "You may have to kill him," he said.

Ryatt knew who he meant. He nodded, his eyes bleak. "Most likely."

Kelly sighed. "I don't envy you."

"You don't have to," Ryatt said evenly. "You're paying me."

Ryatt lingered inside the office after Kelly left, looking the place over. The floor smelled of crinoline, scrubbed boards bleaching. Everything was in order. There was an Atchinson, Topeka & Santa Fe poster on one wall, extolling the virtues of the western plains country — clean air, blue skies, buffalo hunting, deluxe sleeping accommodations, and excellent dining car service. Some old dodgers, yellowing with age, were pinned to the wall next to the boot-scarred rolltop desk. Ryatt recognized some of the men on the wanted posters.

He checked the empty cells, then came back and went through the desk. He pocketed the office keys. A half bottle of some previous occupant's whiskey was tucked away in a bottom drawer, along with some rifle-cleaning rags and old tobacco. But the brass spittoon was clean, recently polished.

Ryatt felt the letdown. Maybe it was the weather, the long, arduous trip up from Santa Fe. His shirt clung to him; there was road dust in his beard stubble. He was a fastidious man; he didn't like being dirty. In the war he had learned to live with it, but he had never become accustomed to it.

He stared bleakly out the window. There was the faint smell of stale tobacco still in this room . . . old sweat, old fears . . .

He went outside, locked up. It was getting dark. A wind scurried bits of paper along the street. In the distance the work train hooted, the sound carrying back to Ryatt. He looked toward the thunderheads boiling up. It was going to be a hell of a storm.

The desk clerk eyed Ryatt as the tall man came up. He looked wilted, sullen. He had an hour yet to go before the night man came on.

He said, "Mr. Ryatt —"

Luke cut him off. He palmed his badge and asked for his room key. The clerk handed it to him.

"Yes, sir, Marshal," he said. "I'll have a man bring hot water for your bath right away."

His gaze followed Ryatt, a sneer spreading across his face. Marshals didn't last long in Dodge. He gave Ryatt less than a week.

Ryatt went up the broad, carpeted stairs. The Dodge House was pretentious. It had an oil painting of Lincoln and others of lesser dignitaries on the wall flanking the staircase. Bracketed oil lamps lighted the upper hallways.

Ryatt's room was midway down the east wing. The door was already open. Sadie Coster was waiting for him, sitting on the edge of the bed. Her trunk was next to her. Her carpetbag was on the side table, her hat hung on one of the brass bedposts, her travel coat draped beside it. She had loosened the top buttons of her high-bodied taffeta dress, and her hair hung loose down her back.

Her voice was bright, cheerful. "You don't mind, do you?"

Ryatt closed the door, took off his dusty black coat, and started to undress.

"Didn't have anywhere to go," she said. She was watching him. "Fifty dollars doesn't take a lady far, anyway."

Ryatt opened his Boston bag, started laying out clean clothes. Lightning suddenly flared viciously. The shock of thunder rattled the windows.

"All I had left, after I paid for Ned's funeral," the girl added.

Ryatt stripped to the buff, picked up his

clean clothes, and tucked them under his arm.

Sadie eyed him appreciatively. "Need help?"

"No."

He went down the hall to the room designated for bathing. There was a cast-iron tub on lion-clawed legs brought in by railroad all the way from Buffalo; it was a feature of the Dodge House. A colored man brought in hot water, soap, and towels.

Ryatt settled himself in the tub. Rain began pattering on the hotel roof as he bathed, coming down hard by the time he finished.

He wiped the steamed-up mirror, shaved, and put on clean clothes. An old wound bothered him a little. He swung his right arm around, loosening muscles.

Sadie was hanging her clothes up in the wardrobe alongside his when Ryatt returned.

He eyed her, admiring her gall.

"You planning to move in?"

She turned and smiled at him. She had a dimple in her left cheek.

"You were Ned Coster's friend, wasn't you?" She said it as though it explained everything.

He shrugged. What the hell? The city was paying for the room . . .

Lightning flared almost constantly now, the rain gusting against closed windows. A prairie thunderstorm was a thing to see!

Ryatt made a bundle of his dirty clothes and handed them to Sadie.

"Earn your keep," he told her. "Get them washed and ironed."

She nodded. "Anything else?"

She was starting to slip out of her dress.

Ryatt grinned. "Not yet."

He strapped his gunbelts around his flat waist, thonged the holsters down, and slipped his derringer inside his waistband.

"What's the toughest hangout in town?"

She stared at him. "The Lady Gay . . ."

He wasn't ready for the Colonel yet.

"Any others?"

"The Green Front Saloon," Sadie said. "Then there's the Comique."

She had worked in all of them.

Ryatt knew where they were. He took out his badge, pinned it on his coat, and checked the tilt of the flat-crowned black hat on his head.

"Where are you going?"

"To work," Ryatt said.

"Jesus!" Sadie muttered. "In this weather?" She sat down on the edge of the bed to wait for him.

5

The town seemed to huddle under the violent thunderstorm. The ankle-deep dust turned to mud, puddles forming between the awning-covered plankwalks. Only a few hardy souls ventured outdoors.

Ryatt kept close to the building wall, getting his boots muddied and his clothes wet only when he cut across the street, beyond the deadline.

He remembered the Green Front Saloon when it had first started doing business in Dodge. It was in a tent then, with a smoking oil lamp hung on a pole outside, a barker wearing a pink silk shirt and a straw hat drumming up business against competition, and the girls, smiles of welcome on painted faces, lined up beside him, waiting. The bar was a plank laid across two empty hogsheads, and the doxies took their customers on straw tick mattresses inside.

Ryatt had come here after the war, a few months after he had gone back home to West Texas to find nothing much remained except two new headboards, those of his father and mother, in the family burial plot.

Dodge was just beginning to boom then, and Front Street was only a wide and muddy place on the Kansas plains. The buffalo still roamed by the thousands across the muddy Arkansas. Ryatt had tried his hand at the buffalo-hide trade, starting as a skinner with the Bill Cody outfit. That was before Cody went back East to become the touted Buffalo Bill.

Ryatt had quit this and worked for a short spell with Bat Masterson and the Earp brothers, shooting buffalo on their own. Masterson he had liked; he had not cared much for the Earps, Wyatt less than Morgan.

The Green Front had come up in the world since then, Ryatt noticed. The tent had been replaced by a two-story wood structure, flat-roofed, weathered, and still unpleasing to the eye.

The rain had gusted against the saloon windows, washing them clean of accumulated prairie grime. A cow-pony nosed the rail, tail to the rain. Ryatt didn't think much of a man who would leave his mount outside on a night like this.

The Green Front was the first south-of-the-deadline watering hole he had come to. The Lady Gay was farther down the street, and so was the Comique. He didn't notice much activity at either place.

He could have waited until morning. But

Ryatt was not a man to waste time on a job, and experience had taught him to come down hard right from the start. Hit one place, close it up. The word would spread, making it easier when he started closing the others.

He pushed the heavy storm door open and stepped inside, pausing to look the place over to see what he was getting into. The saloon was longer than it was wide, with a flight of stairs along the wall leading to rooms behind the balcony railing. Cribs were a better name for them.

It was a slow night in the Green Front. Several of the saloon girls were clustered around the piano player, a thin, balding man with a bowler hat cocked back on his head. He was fingering the keys, letting melodies drift in and out between his fingers.

No one was paying any attention to him or the girls. Most of the tables were empty. A white-haired drunk was asleep over one, the bartender was serving a round of drinks at another. Five men were grouped around it, playing poker. None of them saw Ryatt come inside.

One of the girls did, however. She pulled away from the others, came toward Ryatt, her smile as phony as the greeting in her voice:

"Hi, stranger."

Ryatt gave her a glance. She had a young-old face, tired eyes, and twenty pounds too many in the wrong places. The paint was piled thick, the cheeks too red. She didn't look too bad in lamplight; she'd look worse in daylight.

"Looking for company?"

Ryatt shook his head. She came up closer, slipping an arm through his. "Come on, feller, be a sport."

Then she spotted the badge. She stiffened and pulled away, mouth tightening.

"Jesus . . ."

Ryatt walked to the bar. The bartender had come back. He was sliding his tray under the counter. He said, without looking up at Ryatt: "Yeah . . . what'll you have, mister?"

"That greener you've got stashed under the counter," Ryatt said evenly. "Pick it up, put it on the bar. Nice and careful like."

The bartender straightened, scowling, his voice belligerent.

"What did you say — ?"

He saw Ryatt's badge at the same moment Ryatt's Colt came up, levelled.

"On the bar," Ryatt repeated grimly.

The bartender reached down and came up with a double-barreled shotgun, sixteen gauge, loaded with buckshot. The barrels had been trimmed down to eighteen inches. At close quarters it could blow a man apart. He placed it very carefully in front of Ryatt.

Luke picked it up, made sure both chambers were loaded, and slipped his Colt back into holster.

"Keep out of this," he warned coldly.

He swung away from the bar, carrying the shotgun. The men at the poker table were intent on their cards. No one paid any attention to Dodge City's new marshal.

Ryatt paused, tilted the double barrels toward the ceiling, and pulled one of the triggers.

The blast got immediate attention.

The man nearest him, a thick-shouldered buffalo hunter, cigar clamped between brown-stained teeth, long yellow hair tied in a pony-tail down the back of his greasy buckskin jacket, spun around in his chair. He reached for his sheath knife, snarling:

"What in hell — ?"

Ryatt laid the shotgun across his bullet head. The buffalo hunter sprawled across the table, cards and money spilling to the floor.

The others froze as Ryatt levelled the twin muzzles at them.

"Sorry, gents," Ryatt said coldly. "Game's over. The place is closed."

He kept his eye on the tow-haired kid across the table from him. Couldn't be more than nineteen, maybe twenty. Thin, narrow face scarred by old pockmarks. Trail worn range clothes, a gun in a thonged-down, worn holster. Texas was written all over him. Young, tough, arrogant. Sap running high

. . . with the gun on his hip he owned the world.

Most likely a trail hand too big for his britches, quitting to hang around Dodge after his outfit had gone back.

The others Ryatt judged to be less dangerous. A gambler, probably a house resident, splitting his take with the owner. Dangerous only if you backed him into a corner. A bib-overalled farmer out for a fling. A soldier from Fort Dodge, five miles up the river. His eyes were bloodshot, his tunic unbuttoned. He was old enough to know better, to realize he was jeopardizing his two stripes and an eventual pension, maybe not giving a damn.

"All guns on the table," Ryatt ordered.

He could see the drunk at the far table, only half awake, gaping, wondering what was going on. The girls at the piano were watching, interest sharpening their gaze. It had been a long, dull day.

The bartender remained behind the bar, his craggy face set in a watchful scowl. He had a Colt stashed away, but he didn't figure to use it. He didn't own the place; he only worked here.

For a long moment no one at the poker table moved. Then the soldier broke the ice. He swore softly as he took his Army-issue pistol from his flap-down holster and laid it on the table.

Ryatt turned his gaze to the gambler. The

tinhorn shrugged, reached inside his coat, drew out a small caliber pistol from a shoulder holster, and set it down carefully beside that of the soldier.

The Texas kid leaned back in his chair and studied Ryatt. There was insolence in his gaze, a challenge.

"Who in hell are you?"

Ryatt cocked the hammer on the loaded barrel. He didn't want to kill a man, unless he had to.

"The name's Ryatt," he said. "Luke Ryatt — town marshal."

"Another one?" the kid asked. He shook his head, reached down for his Colt, set it down on the table. It had a walnut butt, rubbed down to a smooth, shiny patina. It was recently oiled. It was probably the most valuable thing the kid owned.

He looked at Ryatt, his grin a sneer: "Last one was planted only last week. You fellers keep coming out of the woodwork . . . ?"

Ryatt ignored him.

The farmer was raising his hands; they were calloused, empty.

"I don't carry a gun," he said. He was a gaunt man, lines like deep furrows down his face. He looked older than he was. He didn't belong here; he was more at home behind a plow.

Ryatt motioned him toward the door. "All right — get out of here! Go on home!"

The farmer stood up, hesitated. He was thinking of his wife. "I . . . I lost thirty dollars . . ." He was looking at the gambler, his lips dry.

"Consider yourself lucky that's all you lost," Ryatt growled.

The farmer backed off reluctantly. Rain was still drumming hard against the saloon windows. It was a long ride home. His mouth pulled down dejectedly as he hitched up his coat collar and went out.

The kid from Texas shifted in his chair as the bartender came out from behind the bar and walked toward them.

"Hey, Monte," he called. "What kind of place you running here?" He turned his sneer to Ryatt. "Who put a goddam badge on this monkey?"

Ryatt knew what would be coming. He leaned across the table and jammed the butt of the shotgun into the kid's face, knocking him backward, out of his chair. The kid started to scramble to his feet, reaching for his gun on the table. He hung there, hand outstretched, staring into the muzzle of the shotgun. Hate flared wildly in his pain-glazed eyes.

"Goddam you, Marshal," he said, spitting blood. "You better kill me now —"

Ryatt cut him off. "That your horse out front?"

The kid didn't answer. He didn't have to.

Couldn't belong to anyone else.

"Any man who'd leave his cayuse out in that rain is a fool," Ryatt snapped. "Anyone from Texas should know better!"

He yanked the kid to his feet and gave him a shove toward the front door. "Get on that horse, and head out of Dodge! *Now!*"

The Texan staggered to the door, then looked back, eyes burning. Humiliation rode him. "I'll be back," he said. His voice was thin, cold, deadly. "Look for me, Marshal. I'll be back!"

He probably would, Ryatt thought, and knew that this went along with the job.

He turned to the soldier. "You can pick up your gun in my office in the morning. There'll be a ten-dollar fine."

"What for?"

"Breaking the law," Ryatt answered. "Carrying a gun inside city limits. Big sign planted right out there in the street. You couldn't miss it."

The gambler stirred, a flicker in his eyes. "That sign was put up a year ago. It reads no guns north of the deadline. This place is south —"

"New town ordinance," Ryatt cut in. His smile was bland. "No guns north or south of the deadline."

He turned to the sullen-mouthed bartender. "I want everybody out tonight. This place is closed!"

The bartender shook his head. "You're crazy! You can't close me! I work for Henry Oliver —"

Ryatt tilted the shotgun toward the bar, blasted the back mirror and shelf bottles into shards of glass.

"I said the place was closed!"

The bartender backed off, white-faced. Ryatt tossed the empty shotgun over the bar, drew his Colt.

"Sorry, girls," he said to the floozies huddled around the piano. "Looks like you'll have to find a new line of work."

The buffalo hunter was beginning to stir. He groaned, putting his head between his hands.

Ryatt motioned to the bartender and the gambler. "Take him to my office. A good night's sleep in jail might sweeten his disposition."

He picked up the guns left behind on the table, the money scattered on the floor. He handed the money to the girls — they'd probably need it.

The storm had passed over Dodge. The rumble of thunder was a diminishing sound.

He had made his point. Law and order had come to Dodge.

It was still to be seen if he could make it stick!

6

It stopped raining during the night. The morning shone bright and clear, a crisp day. Dodge City's board fronts were washed clean; they steamed to the warming rays of the rising sun.

Ryatt stood by the window and watched two men pick their way across the muddy street and head for the law office. He was expecting them.

Down the street, and still within his line of vision, a new board sign had been erected, replacing the old one.

It read:

WARNING!
No weapons to be carried
north or south
of the Deadline!
By order of:
Marshal Luke Ryatt.

The sign had cost the city twenty dollars. Ryatt figured Dodge could afford it.

The two men stormed into the office,

boots muddied, eyes blazing. One of them was Mayor John Kelly. The other was a town man. Tall, gaunt, pale gray eyes, starched white collar, sombre clothes. Thin, ascetic features, a nervous tic under his right eye. Looked like a preacher . . . hell on sin and sex . . .

Kelly slammed the door shut behind them and swung around to Ryatt. "Just what in the devil are you doing?" he fumed. "What the hell's going on, Luke? Closing the Green Front Saloon, bullying the customers, running the girls out on the street —"

Ryatt grinned. "I've been cleaning up the town," he said. "That's what you hired me for, isn't it?"

"Sure." Kelly sounded exasperated. "But nailing saloon doors shut, putting up signs and charging them to the city —"

"Shows you I've been busy."

"Too goddam busy — in the wrong places!" the other man snapped. "You were hired to keep order in town, that's all!" He pointed a stiff, bony finger at Ryatt, his voice harsh. "Now you get your ass back to the Green Front and reopen it! Tell Monte you're sorry. And then keep your hands off the place!"

Ryatt turned to Mayor Kelly. "Who's he?"

"Henry Oliver." The Mayor was calming down. "Henry owns the Green Front."

"You don't say." Ryatt ran his gaze up and

down the tall, angry man. "Figured him for a sky pilot."

Oliver's thin lips pursed. "Maybe you didn't hear me, Ryatt. I want my place re-opened — now!"

Ryatt's eyes went cold. "Why don't you do it, mister? Go ahead. Take a walk across the deadline and pry those boards off the Green Front door. You go ahead and try it, Mister Oliver —"

Oliver's pale eyes glittered. "And —"

"I'll slap you in jail!"

The tall man suppressed a cold rage. "You fool! It'll take me just thirty minutes to walk up the street and get a court injunction —"

Ryatt cut him off. "The Green Front stays closed. You go ahead — get your injunction." His grin was cold, sardonic. 'Let's make it plain all over Dodge who owns the place, who's behind the gambling and the crib girls south of the deadline . . ."

Oliver trembled, his face paling with fury. He turned his frustration on Kelly.

"You hired him, John!" His voice was barely above a whisper. "Now you get rid of him! You hear me? Get rid of the bastard before he . . . he . . ."

Words failed him. He swung around and slammed the door behind him as he stamped out. Kelly sighed. He looked at Ryatt and shook his head. "You had to do it?"

Ryatt nodded.

"Why didn't you start with the Lady Gay? That's where most of the trouble is. That's where the Colonel and his men hang out."

"I'll come to him later," Ryatt said. He moved away from the window. "Last night was just for openers. I'm not stopping with the Green Front. I'm going to close every saloon and whorehouse south of the dead-line —"

Kelly exploded. "You're crazy!"

"You want this town clean?"

"What are you?" Kelly demanded angrily, "Some Boston bluenose? Case you don't know it, drinking is still legal in Dodge City, and so is prostitution —"

"And making money from it is most legal of all!" Ryatt shrugged. "Look — I don't give a damn what you do after I leave. You can reopen the Green Front, the Lady Gay, all the whorehouses. Turn loose the shills, the con men, and the gamblers again. Let every two-bit gunman who comes up the trail swagger through town, a gun on his hip and a pea brain behind it. If that's what you want, fine! But while I'm here the town stays clean, John! That's what the fifteen thousand dollars is getting you!"

Kelly frowned. "Well, I guess you have a point. Sooner or later all towns will come to that, anyway. There's a lot of decent people in Dodge — they'll want it that way."

He walked to the door and turned, his lips

quirking wryly. "There's a rumor going around that you're living with a woman. Ned Coster's widow?"

Ryatt nodded. "She takes care of things for me."

"Yeah — I'll bet," the Mayor said.

Ryatt grinned. "I've only been in town two days, but I've been hearing rumors, too, Mayor. Like about a woman by the name of Mady Williams . . . ?"

Mayor Kelly flushed.

"Your wife's name Mady?"

"None of your goddam business!" Kelly snarled. His feathers were ruffled. Anger reddened his pink face. "Don't forget, Ryatt — I gave you the badge you're wearing on your coat, and I can take it off!"

"You can — but you won't," Ryatt said calmly. He pointed toward the window.

"Stick around, Mayor. We've got more company coming."

Morry Teague slammed his way into the law office and glared at Kelly and Ryatt. He was wearing town clothes, pants tucked inside high leather boots, and a Remington .44 pistol thrust inside his waistband.

"They raided me last night! Broke into my holding pens, stampeded the stock. A thousand head of cattle scattered between hell and gone."

He paused to get his breath and take control. He jutted his chin at Ryatt. "You hear that, Marshal? A thousand head . . . most of them prime fed, ready for shipment to Chicago meat packers!"

Ryatt shrugged. "Looks like a job for the county sheriff —"

"Sheriff, hell!" Morry shook his finger under Ryatt's nose. "What in hell do you think we're paying you for?"

"Not to go out chasing your stampeded beef," Ryatt answered mildly.

"You'll ride where I tell you!" Morry snarled. "And you'll jump when I say so! Or by hell —" He took a step back, his big shoulders hunching, eyes glittering dangerously, his right hand coming up toward his gun.

Ryatt slouched, waiting . . . his eyes deadly.

"Jesus Christ!" Kelly stepped between them, sweating. "Goddammit, calm down, Morry — calm down!" He turned to face Ryatt. "It's not an unreasonable request, Luke. Morry's holding pens are within city limits. He's entitled to protection, same as any other merchant in town."

Ryatt nodded, easing. "Same as anybody else," he growled. "No more, no less."

Morry quieted down, his anger, however, only barely leashed.

"All right, then — what are you going to do about it?"

"Who raided you?"

61

"I wasn't there," Morry answered. He had gained control of himself and was the more dangerous because of it. Ryatt judged him correctly . . . a big man, ambitious, used to getting his own way. And that gun in his waistband was not just for show . . . Morry could use it, if pushed.

"My men didn't get a good look at them," Morry was saying. "They weren't expecting trouble, what with that storm hitting us last night."

"Anyone hurt?"

"One of my hands was killed. Two wounded." Morry's lips twitched coldly. "We thought they were Indians, at first. Kiowas, or Cheyenne . . ."

"Could have been," Ryatt interjected.

"Yeah — could have," Morry said grimly. "Until one of my men found *this* this morning."

He reached into his pocket and took out a muddy, still-wet Confederate forage cap. He tossed it to Ryatt.

Kelly said: "The Colonel?"

"Who else? The sonuvabitch's been itching to get back at me ever since the day I bought his beef!"

He swung around to face Ryatt, his eyes boring into the marshal's. "I hear you were out last night, closing up the Green Front?"

Ryatt nodded.

"That was a helluva waste of time," Morry

said harshly. "I told you where the trouble was. Waiting for you, right there in the Lady Gay. That's what I voted to pay for, Ryatt. I want those goddam, trigger-happy, thieving Texans run out of Dodge!" A sneer rode his lips. "If you're half as good as Ned Coster boasted you were, it shouldn't be any trouble."

Ryatt's smile was bleak. "No trouble at all."

"What are you waiting for?"

"Proof," Ryatt answered coolly. He took a slim cigar from his vest pocket, snapped a match to flame on his thumbnail, and lighted up. "I like to know why, before I kill a man."

Morry Teague's eyes narrowed angrily. "I just told you who raided me. That cap's all the proof you need. Now get the hell out there and do your job!"

He turned, started to stride out of the office. Ryatt's voice stopped him. Flat. Cold.

"Just a minute!"

Morry turned slowly.

"Your gun."

Morry stiffened.

"You read the sign out there," Ryatt said. "I'm making no exceptions."

Morry smiled. It was a small, deadly smile . . . a man pushed too far.

"You want my gun, Marshal . . . you come and get it!"

Ryatt brushed his coat back from his holster gun. "No exceptions," he repeated flatly.

Morry's gun hand quivered. The silence hung in that room, strained, deadly. It was broken by Mayor Kelly's sudden gasp:

"Morry! For Christ's sakes, Morry — *give him your gun!*"

Slowly the big man's weight came down off his toes. His breath expelled in a sudden gust of spent anger. His fingers reached for his gun, slowly, carefully. He lifted the Remington . . .

"On the desk," Ryatt instructed grimly.

Morry took a step forward and dropped the gun on Ryatt's desk.

"You staying in town?"

The big man nodded, not trusting his voice.

"Pick it up when you leave."

Morry backed off, looking at Kelly. His face showed strain, a condemning bitterness.

"You hired him, John. I hope to hell we won't all be sorry!"

Kelly waited until Morry left before speaking. He was still shaken by what might have happened.

"Would you have killed him?"

Ryatt shrugged. "If I had to."

Kelly sat down, mopping cold sweat from his face. "I don't understand you," he muttered. "You were hired because the toughs in town were getting out of hand. But so far all you've done is antagonize Henry Oliver and Morry Teague —"

"I told you I might be stepping on some toes," Ryatt interrupted. He picked up Morry's Remington and shoved it inside one of the desk drawers.

Kelly's Irish temper flared. "Goddammit, that isn't what I had in mind!" He pointed to the muddy forage cap on the desk. "Morry was right. There's your proof. Or are you stalling because those men are Texans, like you? Because the man who calls himself the Colonel was once your C.O.?"

Kelly had a point. There was an inner reluctance in Ryatt he had not quite faced up to.

He picked up the gray forage cap, old memories stirring. The flash and thunder of field pieces . . . a tall, gaunt man striding across a desolated battlefield, moving forward, unafraid, determined . . .

Kelly's voice drove a wedge into the old memories. "I'm sorry, Luke. What's past is past. There is no north or south here . . . no war. Just the law, and the lawbreakers. And as long as you're wearing that badge —"

"You'll get what you're paying for," Ryatt said. "A clean town — and a quiet one."

He picked up the Confederate forage cap. "I'll go see the Colonel, Kelly."

7

"Yeah," Sadie said in answer to Ryatt's question, "Jeff Corby was killed about two weeks ago. Got into a gunfight at the Lady Gay. Just a couple of days after the Colonel and his men came to Dodge."

She and Ryatt were in the Dodge House dining room, at a window table. The waiter serving them was chilly, aloof — a cold, repressed man in his middle forties, hair thinning, sallow-faced.

Sadie noticed, but didn't care. Ryatt paid the man no attention.

"I was there," Sadie said. She was munching on a biscuit, a touch of raspberry jam staining her lips. "That was before the Texans took the place over. I saw Corby get killed. Don't remember how it started, though. I was with the other girls, working . . ."

"Who shot him?"

"One of the Colonel's men. Big, raunchy cowhand, built like a bull." She giggled at this, sobered at Ryatt's frown. "I remember seeing Jeff talking to him. Whatever he said didn't seem to set well with Rafe. I think that was his name."

"Rafe?" Ryatt searched back in his memory, couldn't place the man.

"Corby wasn't very good with a gun, was he?" Sadie asked.

"No," Ryatt answered. "He wasn't."

He finished his coffee. "I knew Coster was living out here," he said slowly. "He never mentioned Jeff in his letters." Ryatt grinned wryly. "Not that Ned was much of a letter-writer."

But it was strange, he thought. He, Ned Coster, and Jeff Corby had been friends. They had gone through a lot together. Four years fighting for a lost cause, going through hell together.

"Jeff owned a small farm just outside of town, up by Walnut Creek," Sadie volunteered. "That is, he did own it."

The waiter came up and stood stiffly to one side of Sadie.

"Anything else? Pie, pudding . . . ?"

His gaze was fixed on Sadie's dress, three buttons open, showing enough cleavage to bother him.

Luke glanced at Sadie. She sighed. "I think I'd better quit while I'm still ahead."

The waiter lingered for one last look, then left.

"Jeff's wife is staying in town, living with her sister," Sadie went on. "They had two small children, a boy and a girl. She shipped them back to her folks in St. Louis."

"But she stayed?" There was interest in Ryatt's tone.

Sadie put more jam on another biscuit. "Yeah. Just waiting to sell the farm, I guess. She can't run it alone."

"Anyone living at the place now?"

"Not that I know of."

Ryatt lighted one of his slim cigars and leaned back. "Why did Ned Coster go to Jeff's place the day he died?"

Sadie wiped her lips with a table napkin. "I don't know. I remember asking him where he was going that day. He said something about going back to the farm to look for something hidden there —"

"Something hidden?" Ryatt frowned. "You know what it was?"

Sadie shook her head. "Ned didn't say. Acted kinda mysterious about it. But he did say that whatever it was, it was going to make him rich."

That didn't sound like a man down on his luck, thinking of taking his life.

"What was it? Money?"

"I wouldn't know. I didn't take him seriously. No one did." Sadie shrugged. "Ned was always going to strike it rich somewhere. He cadged more drinks that way."

The waiter came up with the tab. Ryatt signed it.

Sadie was reaching for another biscuit. Ryatt took it away from her.

"Let's go before that waiter comes back for another look."

Sadie ran her hand down her unbuttoned dress front. "Oh, you noticed?"

"Who wouldn't?"

Sadie took a biscuit with her as they went out. In the lobby, Ryatt asked, "Where can I find Jeff's wife?"

Sadie's eyes darkened. "Why?"

"None of your business," Ryatt said.

She pouted. "She hasn't got anything I don't have . . . and in some places a whole lot less."

Ryatt grinned. "Is that all you can think of?"

"What else is there?"

"Try church."

Sadie watched him leave, her eyes clouding. She didn't notice the man sitting behind the potted palm in the lobby until she turned and started to go upstairs.

Morry Teague tossed the newspaper aside and went after her. He caught her by the arm before she reached the middle landing. Looking back, she winced, her face paling.

"Getting up in the world, Sadie?" Morry's voice held a thin sneer.

She ran her tongue across her full lips. "Morry, please!" She smothered a cry of pain as his thick fingers dug into her arm.

"Well . . ."

"He . . . he's still asking questions about Coster," she said. "And Jeff Corby." She hated him for making her do this, but she had no choice.

"Where's he going now?"

"To see Amy Corby."

Morry frowned. "Why?"

"I don't know." Sadie bit her lips at the look in Morry's eyes. "I swear I don't know."

"Find out!" Morry ordered coldly. "Get him to talk. You're good at that, Sadie."

He released his grip on her arm. "Remember, a hundred dollar bonus and a through ticket to Denver. If you're a good little girl, Sadie."

He waited, watching her go the rest of the way upstairs.

Amy Corby said icily: "No, I'm afraid Jeff never mentioned you, Mr. Ryatt. He didn't talk much about the war. I'm afraid he found little pleasure in it."

She was standing in the doorway of a small cottage in Dodge's better residential district . . . a slender, patrician looking woman nudging thirty. Ash blonde hair, green eyes tinged with flecks of gold. Cold eyes, level and direct now, holding Ryatt off.

She was dressed in black, as befitting a recent widow. A beautiful woman once, Ryatt judged . . . could still be, once she loosened up again.

70

"Can't say that I blame him," Ryatt replied. He looked past her, down a short hallway. The house was quiet. If there was anyone else inside, they were making themselves scarce.

"May I come in, Mrs. Corby?"

Amy hesitated. "I'm sorry. I'm not up to seeing people."

"Just for a minute," Ryatt promised. "I won't overstay my visit."

She stepped back reluctantly, and Ryatt followed her down the hallway into a stiffly furnished sitting room. She didn't take his hat, didn't ask him to sit.

"I understand you've sent your children to St. Louis, Mrs. Corby?"

"Yes." Her eyes searched him, a slight frown darkening the golden flecks. "As soon as I sell the farm, I'm joining them."

"Any buyers?"

Amy's gaze looked through him. There was nothing colder than a beautiful woman, Ryatt thought —

"Why?"

"I might be interested."

Her gaze sighted in on his badge; her lips curled in disbelief.

"Luke Ryatt — a farmer?"

"So you have heard of me?"

Her face smoothed, went stiff, cold. "Ned Coster talked about you," she admitted. She sat across from him now, hands folded primly

71

in her lap. "Oh, yes, Ned visited." From the tone of her voice Ryatt guessed she didn't like old Coster.

"An unpleasant man," she continued. "Chewed tobacco, was careless where he spit . . ." She shuddered a little. "But I did feel sorry for him. There are not many things a one-armed man can do to earn a living, is there?"

"No," Ryatt said levelly. "Not many."

She leaned forward, eyes searching him, trying to understand why Ryatt was here, what he wanted of her.

"Did Jeff ever mention anything about money . . . some scheme he might have been involved in with Ned Coster . . . ?"

"Scheme?"

Ryatt smiled. "Well, business deal?"

"No." She stood up again, facing Ryatt. "Ned Coster was a bad influence on Jeff. He drank too much, gambled, frequented the . . . the sporting houses in town. I didn't like him. My husband knew it —"

"What was Jeff doing in the Lady Gay, the night he was killed?"

It hurt. It showed in her face, in her eyes . . . a sharp, bitter hurt.

"I don't know," she said stiffly. "I thought Jeff was happy at home. I . . ."

She walked Ryatt back to the front door.

"Perhaps you know," she said quietly. "Maybe you know why Jeff would want to go to . . . to a place like that, Mr. Ryatt?"

He could guess, but he'd never tell her. After all, he might be wrong.

He touched his hat. "Good day, Mrs. Corby."

8

Luke Ryatt went back to the law office and picked up the Confederate forage cap Morry Teague had brought in. He had promised Kelly he'd follow it up. It was time, anyway, to pay the Colonel a visit.

The Kid was waiting for him when Ryatt stepped out of the office. He was standing by the board sign, his cowpony hitched to it, standing slack-hipped in the afternoon sun.

"Marshal!" the Kid called sharply. "Remember me?"

Ryatt paused.

Men and women were out on the plank-walks, going about their business. But the Kid stood alone out in the wide, muddy street, the Santa Fe rails behind him, gleaming in the sun. Pock-faced, lips still puffed, a greasy coat hanging loosely on narrow shoulders.

Somewhere he had spent the night . . . somewhere he had picked up another gun. It lay snuggled in his holster, ready to be used. A challenge. An answer to his humiliation . . . a deadly sop to his bruised ego.

"I've been waiting for you," the Kid said.

Ryatt glanced down the street. He was on his way to the Lady Gay . . . it was time. But he would have to get by this trigger-happy kid first. There was no way he could avoid it.

Ryatt hesitated, watching the puddle in front of the Kid, the sun shining in it. The reflection bothered him. The deadline lay just beyond. He could see a man standing in front of the Lady Gay, watching. It was not the Colonel.

People were stopping on the plankwalks, moving out of the line of direct fire, looking on.

The Kid knew he had an audience; it was what he wanted. He stood by the board sign, worn boots muddied, hands hanging down by his sides.

"I'm wearing a gun, Marshal," the Kid taunted. "What are you going to do about it?"

Ryatt stepped down into the street, moved off at an angle, then stopped. The sun no longer reflected from the puddle, into his eyes.

It had to be, Ryatt thought bleakly. *Best to get it over with. Fast.*

The Kid stepped away from the board sign, stiff-legged now, a grotesque grin on his puffed lips. A thin, gangly kid, big ears sticking out from under his greasy hat.

"Name's Nelson," he said. "Orly Nelson!"

He said it loudly. He wanted everyone within earshot to know who he was.

Regret made its brief run through Ryatt and was replaced by irritation. Talking wouldn't do any good. It never did. Not with kids like this . . . punks with a fast gun, looking for a reputation.

"You want my iron," the Kid called. "Well, come on and get it!"

Ryatt studied him.

Forty feet of muddy road separated them . . . forty feet and eleven years . . . and a war in between.

The Kid licked his lips now, uncertainty flickering in his eyes. He was used to talk, to bluster . . . not a cold, studied silence.

"Cat got your tongue, Marshal?"

It was useless, Ryatt knew, but he had to try. Just once.

"Don't be a fool, kid," he said. "Check your gun, have your fun in town, pick it up when you leave."

It was a mistake. The uncertainty flickered out of the young Texan's pale gaze. His grin grew insolent, his voice arrogant. The marshal of Dodge City was backing down . . .

"Ain't nobody gonna take my gun," he said. "Nobody in this goddam town."

His right hand jerked to his holstered gun.

Ryatt shot him.

The Kid staggered, fell. He fell face down in the puddle, right hand bent under him, holding a gun he had managed to draw, but never got to fire.

Ryatt walked up to him and looked down at the small, thin figure for a long moment. He had seen bodies lying in the mud before. Lots of them. Seen them piled on slopes of wooded ridges, wearing blue and gray uniforms. Most of them young, like this kid . . . some of them less than bodies. Some of them only pieces of what once had been men.

Slowly Ryatt slipped his Colt back into its holster and turned away.

9

The man who had been watching Ryatt from in front of the Lady Gay had gone back inside. Ryatt pushed the door open and stepped in. He knew they were waiting for him.

The place was quiet, sunlight slanting in through the windows. Once one of Dodge City's rowdier watering holes, it now seemed almost deserted. The gaming tables were pushed up against the far wall, gathering dust. The girls who had given the saloon its name were gone, the upstairs rooms pre-empted, taken over by the men from Texas. There was no piano player. A man wearing a forage cap tended bar.

The Colonel was seated at a table, flanked by two men. He was older than Ryatt remembered, thinner . . . a man living more within himself. Even sitting he still managed to retain a military bearing. There was no insignia on his old gray tunic, but somehow silver oak leaves seemed to be pinned there, on his shoulders.

Three other men watched from another

corner of the room, legs sprawled out, no sign of tension. Hard men, armed, confident.

The Colonel had a bottle in front of him, a half-filled glass. He stirred as Ryatt walked across the room and said casually: "It's been a long time, Luke. Pickett's Mill, wasn't it?"

Ryatt nodded.

The Colonel waved him to a chair. The big man beside him watched Ryatt, a sneer on his broad face.

"Sit down," the Colonel said. "We've got a lot to talk over."

"I'll stand," Ryatt said coldly.

The Colonel shrugged. "You never did take orders well, I remember."

"No," Ryatt answered, unsmiling. "I never did."

The Colonel's long fingers shuffled cards absently between them. He was wearing a shoulder holster, a .38 Smith & Wesson. But he still carried an Army-issue Colt .45 in a military holster at his side. Maybe this was just a habit, a carryover from his military days. Ryatt judged the .38 would be the gun he would get to first.

"You're late," the Colonel said. "I've been expecting you ever since I heard you had come to town."

The big man beside the Colonel said: "Yeah — we all heard of you." His sneer stretched across his unshaven face. "Luke Ryatt — town tamer!"

Ryatt ran his gaze slowly over the big man. "Your name Rafe?"

The man's gaze flickered, thick lips curling. "You heard of me, eh?"

Ryatt nodded slowly. The man who killed Jeff Corby. He'd remember that.

The Colonel was frowning, his cold gaze locking on Ryatt's badge.

"They gave you a tin star, Luke. What do they want of you?"

"The town wants you out," Ryatt replied levelly. The sunlight slanting in through the windows laid a rough splotch on the worn floor boards. The room was quiet. He didn't know any of these other men. The bartender was watching him from behind the bar.

"You and your men," Ryatt went on. "They want you out of Dodge, or —"

He let it hang. But the Colonel said coldly: "Or what, Luke?"

"You go out," Luke Ryatt said grimly, "one way or the other!"

"Wal, now . . ." Rafe said, drawing in his legs, starting to get up. "Tell me that again, Marshal."

The Colonel pulled him back into his chair.

"We fought together, Luke," the Colonel said. "We believed in the same things, once." His long fingers riffled through the deck, stacking cards. He placed the deck down on the table in front of him.

"I'll cut cards with you, Luke. For old

times sakes. For the times we took a hill, and the times we lost a battle." He went quiet, remembering. But when his eyes lifted to Luke again they were cold, unfriendly.

"High card, I stay. Low card, you go."

Ryatt shook his head. "Sorry, Morgan. No games."

The Colonel leaned across the table, anger glowing in his eyes now. "So the town wants me out? Who's the town, Luke? Morry Teague?"

"You raided him last night."

The Colonel pulled back and smiled. "Prove it."

Ryatt reached inside his coat pocket, took out the muddy forage cap Morry had brought him, and tossed it on the table.

Rafe said, sneering: "Wal, lookit that!" He turned to his younger companion. "Looks like your headgear, Barney. Kinda messed up some."

The man called Barney looked to be not much older than the kid, Orly Nelson, Ryatt had just killed. Straw hair, pale gray eyes, a rider's wiriness. Too young to have been in the war. He couldn't have ridden with Morgan. But he was wearing a Confederate forage cap, like the rest of the Colonel's men. A reminder perhaps, of a war lost — but not surrendered!

"Yeah," Barney said, picking it up, looking at Ryatt. "Where'd you find it, Marshal?"

Ryatt ignored him.

"You know how it is, Morgan," Ryatt said. "I took this job . . . I'm getting paid. Because we did ride together once, I'm going to give you until tomorrow night to get your things together and get out of Dodge."

His gaze swung around to Rafe and Barney, rifling to the other Texans in the saloon.

"All of you," he said bluntly. "Out — by tomorrow night!"

They watched Luke Ryatt standing there, a tall, hard man in a long, black coat, flat-crowned black hat. Two guns showing, thonged down. Some of them remembered him; most of them didn't.

He was standing there, one man . . . one man telling them they had twenty-four hours to get out of town! One man, alone, facing them. They admired his gall; it wouldn't stop them from killing him.

Rafe shoved his chair back hard, his hand starting for his gun. The Colonel stopped him . . . his voice flat, hard.

"No, Rafe!"

Rafe hesitated, looked sullen, and slid slowly back into his chair.

"Let me tell you why I won't be leaving," the Colonel said. "Something you should know before taking that badge too seriously, Luke." He paused, fingers drumming on the table. "I came here with a thousand head.

You know what that meant to me? Five years of hard work . . . five years putting the pieces together on a rundown ranch. Fighting reconstruction, drought, maverickers. Five years trying to start all over again, trying to forget a war we lost. That's what I put into that trail herd, Luke — blood, sweat, and hope. All the way up the Chisum Trail we heard the going price for Texas beef was between fifteen to twenty dollars a head. That's what I expected to get." He leaned back, eyes grim: "But that wasn't what I got, Luke —"

"You had a choice," Ryatt pointed out. "You didn't have to sell."

"Like hell I didn't!" The Colonel stood up, facing Ryatt. "We got here fighting Indians, eating dust. We lived on beans and hardtack. We fought storms and stampedes. When we got here we were out of food, out of money. And there was only one buyer — Morry Teague! Eight dollars a head! Take it or leave it!"

He paused — a cough racked him for a moment, leaving him pale-faced.

"Sure," he said, his voice low now, strained. "Sure, I could have said to hell with him. But I knew we couldn't make it to Abilene, not in the shape we were in."

He settled back in his chair, shaking his head. "We're staying, Luke. And we're going to keep on raising hell here, until Morry

Teague pays us what he owes."

"You took his money," Ryatt cut in, "you signed a bill of sale. According to the law, he's in the clear."

"Not my law," the Colonel said.

Ryatt shrugged. "Sorry, Morgan. I've got no choice. Twenty-four hours! Take it, and leave!"

The Colonel's eyes showed a hint of regret. "I never liked you, Luke. But you were a damn good soldier, once."

He picked up the deck and slid the cards face down across the tab table.

"Because of that, because you're a Texan, I'm letting you walk out of here. I'm turning your offer around. I'm giving you twenty-four hours to turn in that badge, and get the hell out of Dodge!"

It was a standoff. Behind Ryatt the red glow on the floorboards faded. The room suddenly seemed gloomy, cold.

"We never did see eye to eye on things," Ryatt said quietly. "And I guess you never did understand me, Morgan."

"You'll be back then?"

Ryatt nodded. "Tomorrow night . . . this time . . ."

The Colonel sighed. "Who sent for you?" he murmured. "Coster?"

"Did you kill him?"

The Colonel's head came up, his eyes meeting Ryatt's, a small, amused smile showing.

"Ned Coster was a fool," the Colonel said. "And Jeff . . ." He shrugged. "It was a mistake, his coming in here."

"Tell me," Ryatt asked bleakly, "what's at the Corby farm, Morgan. What's out there you want bad enough to kill two old soldiers for?"

The Colonel ran his fingers down the spread-out cards. He picked one out, turned it over, and flipped it out to Ryatt. It fell to the floor, face up — the ace of spades.

"You tell me, Luke," he said softly. "What is out there?"

10

The woman who came to the door of the Mayor's house was about thirty-five. She looked older, her hair graying. But she had eyes that laughed, a mouth that smiled readily, and a figure best described as comfortable.

She looked out at Ryatt waiting on the stoop and said: "Yes . . . ?" in a voice that was half invitation.

"Mrs. Kelly?"

The woman laughed. "No. I'm Mady Williams . . . the Mayor's housekeeper."

"Is Mayor Kelly in?"

There was a lamp shining somewhere behind her, outlining her figure. She didn't look like she was doing any housekeeping. Not the usual kind, anyway. She was wearing a robe over a nightgown and her hair was unpinned; she was a woman ready for bed, or already in bed, although it was still early in the evening.

"No." She was smiling. She knew he knew she was lying, and she didn't care. In fact, it seemed to amuse her.

"You might try the Long Branch Saloon —"

"I have."

She shrugged then, looking Ryatt over. There was a complete frankness to her gaze. She liked what she saw — she showed it.

"Can I be of help, Marshal?"

"Some other time," he answered. Mayor Kelly, he thought, had his hands full with this woman.

"Yes," she said, lowering her voice. "Some other time . . ."

She watched Ryatt walk back to the street before she closed the door, turned, and slipped out of her robe. Her breasts were full. They jiggled under the nightgown as she went down the hallway to the Mayor's bedroom . . .

Ryatt walked slowly back along the street toward the Dodge House. It was now quite dark. Dodge City was quiet. He had closed the Green Front and made it stick . . . he had warned the others. The bars and whorehouses south of the deadline had pulled in their horns . . . they were waiting to see how long this would last. If this new town marshal was for real.

They wouldn't have to wait long.

Ryatt had given himself until tomorrow night. The town would be cleaned up. That's what he had promised . . . that's what Dodge City would get. What happened afterward was none of his concern.

There was a light shining in the windows of the *Dodge City Gazette*. On impulse, Ryatt cut across the street. Maybe Fred Gelson would know what he had gone to see the Mayor about.

The publisher was in his cubbyhole office, blue-pencilling copy. Outside, the flatbed press was silent. Gelson's printer, a white-haired man, was sorting out lead slugs, getting ready to set up type.

The small man looked up as Ryatt stepped inside his office.

"Just in time," he said. He leaned back in his swivel chair, shoved his green eyeshade up on his forehead, and grinned. "I'm writing your obit. Need a little more information — like next of kin —"

"A bit premature," Ryatt said, matching Gelson's grin. "You could be sued for libel."

Gelson shrugged. "A good newspaperman has to keep ahead of the news." He shook his head. "For Chrissakes, Ryatt — two days on the job and already you've got the Mayor on your back, Henry Oliver after your scalp, and Morry Teague gunning for you!"

"How do you feel?"

"Me?" Gelson picked up the copy in front of him and tossed it to Ryatt. "Read it. Closing the bars and whorehouses south of the deadline is going too far, Ryatt. I know we agreed to back you. But that — hell, that's not even legal!"

"I didn't do it because it was legal — just necessary."

Gelson frowned. "I don't know whether to admire your brashness," he admitted, "or dismiss you as a plain goddam fool."

"Do me a favor instead," Ryatt said, smiling. He sat on the edge of the newspaper man's desk. "Won't cost you anything."

"Why should I?"

"You want a story? I'll give you one. Front page stuff, no charge."

Gelson's eyes showed a tired, cynical interest. "Go ahead."

"I've just come from the Lady Gay." Ryatt continued. "I gave the Colonel and his men twenty-four hours to get out of Dodge."

Gelson laughed. "You expect him to go?"

"No."

Gelson frowned and rubbed the tip of his nose. He eased back in his chair, studying Ryatt.

"Well . . . ?"

"So, tomorrow night I earn my fifteen thousand dollar fee, or . . ." Ryatt smiled grimly, "you get to print that obit."

"That's what Mayor Kelly said. By the way, I went to see his Honor."

"He wasn't at home?"

"He was, but . . ."

"Oh!" Gelson reached inside a desk drawer and took out a bottle and two glasses.

"You met John's housekeeper?"

"Yeah." Ryatt grinned. "Quite a handful." He shrugged. "Early to bed, early to rise . . ."

"Keeps Kelly a reasonably happy man," Gelson said, capping it for Ryatt. He poured and handed the marshal a glass. "Sorry, no champagne. Pretty good bourbon, though."

He leaned back in his chair, eyeing Ryatt. "What do you want to know?"

"Did Kelly tell you I served with the Colonel? He was a Captain then, and my commanding officer?"

Gelson nodded.

"Rode to San Antone, joined up," Ryatt said. "That's where I met Ned Coster. And Jeff Corby. We went through the war together. They were both older. They sort of took me under their wing."

Gelson remained silent, waiting.

"Makes my coming here a sort of reunion," Ryatt said. "Would have, if Ned and Jeff were still alive."

The newspaperman scowled. "You sure you want to go through with this?"

Ryatt shrugged. "Like I told Kelly, the war's over. But Ned Coster was a friend, and Corby, too."

He finished his bourbon and stood up.

"Jeff was killed in the Lady Gay. He had a wife, kids, a farm. He wasn't the kind of man to go looking for his fun in a whorehouse. He must have gone there for another reason."

"You think to see the Colonel?"

"Maybe. I thought you — or Kelly — might know why."

Fred Gelson shook his head. "Jeff got in a gunfight there and was shot. That's all I know. I don't believe Kelly knows any different. But if you should find out why Jeff went there —"

"Yeah," Ryatt cut in, frowning. "That's what Mrs. Corby said, too."

He was silent for a moment, thinking. Then: "Ned Coster wired me to come. Said it was urgent —"

"Sure. The town was getting out of hand, the merchants hurting. The last marshal we hired left town suddenly. We needed someone fast. We couldn't call on the soldiers at Fort Dodge, and the sheriff is located forty miles from here. So when Ned Coster told us you could handle the job —"

"And a couple of days later he was killed." Ryatt put up his hand, forestalling the newspaperman's reply. "Yeah — I know. Suicide. Because Coster was found hanging at the Corby farm. Nobody there except old Ned. Feeling sorry about his friend Jeff being killed in the Lady Gay. So he climbs up into Jeff's loft, loops a rope around his neck and over a beam and hangs himself."

"That's the story I printed," Gelson said.

"I don't believe it, Fred. Not Ned Coster. One-armed or no, Ned wasn't buying out of this life. Someone would have to kill him first."

"I said I printed it," Gelson replied. "I

didn't say I believed it."

"Besides," Ryatt went on, "Ned had just taken himself a wife." He frowned. "He did marry her, didn't he?"

Gelson smiled. "He did. A doxie name of Sadie. Used to cadge drinks, and customers, in the Lady Gay before the Colonel took the place over. She'd sell out her mother for two bits . . ." He paused, studied Ryatt, made an offhand gesture. "I hear she's staying with you . . ."

"It bother you?"

"Why should it? That's your business, Marshal." The newspaper publisher leaned forward. "Can't figure you out, though. You close the whorehouses, but you live with one —"

"Don't try!"

Ryatt eased off Gelson's desk and walked to the door. "What's out at the Corby place anyone would want, Fred? Want badly enough to kill two men for?"

"Jeff's farm?" Gelson scowled. "One hundred and sixty acres of prairie grass, half of it ploughed for crops. A few milk cows, some beef cattle, a few chickens, and some hogs. Used to sell his meat to the local butcher —"

"Worth?"

"Ten dollars an acre, throw in the house and the livestock," Gelson muttered. "Fifteen would be too high."

"Looks like killing comes cheap here,"

Ryatt muttered. "Unless . . ." He shrugged, letting it go.

He reached for the doorknob. "Hold that obit, Fred?"

The newspaperman nodded. "Couple of things I feel you should know, Marshal. That Texas trailhand named Orly Nelson, the one you just —"

Ryatt cut him off. "What about the kid?"

"Came up the trail about a couple of months ago. Had words with his ramrod and shot him. Hung around town after that, swaggering his way in and out of the joints south of the deadline. Killed two other men, then shot Frank Chase, the town marshal. Frank had friends, so the kid left town right after." Gelson shrugged. "Last night was the first time he'd been back."

"Texan?"

Gelson nodded. "Not with the Colonel's crowd, though. And no kin, far as I could make out."

Ryatt shrugged.

"The kid was asking to be killed," Gelson went on. "But he's just the beginning. There'll be others coming to test that ordinance."

"Part of the job," Ryatt said. His voice was even.

"That buffalo hunter you skulled in the Green Front. Name's Rego Larsen. Mean sonuvabitch. Most of these goddam buffalo

93

hunters are. Doctor Hayden put ten stitches in his scalp. Rego left town early this morning. I figure he'll be back — with friends."

Ryatt smiled. "Thanks for telling me."

"They won't be checking their guns," Gelson warned. "And they won't be standing out in the middle of Front Street, like that Texas kid, waiting for you . . ."

Ryatt's grin was cold. "Neither will I!"

11

Sadie was on her hands and knees, going through Ryatt's suitcase when Luke stepped into the room. She turned, looked up at him, startled . . . then innocence flooded her eyes. Dark, lustrous, glistening too brightly.

Her mouth parted in a small gasp of relief. "You frightened me, Luke. I thought you were a prowler —"

She was wearing one of Ryatt's white shirts, nothing else. It didn't cover much.

He closed the door. "Find what you were looking for?"

She got to her feet. His shirttails came almost to her knees.

"Gee, I hope you don't mind. I wanted to surprise you."

"You did."

She walked up to him, smiling coquettishly. "I'm hungry."

He looked down at his shirt. "Is that the way you dress for dinner?"

She made a face.

"I was just trying it on." She ran the palm of her hand slowly down over the front of his shirt, over the bulge of a breast. "I love a man's shirt," she said. "It feels so masculine."

Ryatt smiled as he slid his hand up the front of the shirt, up to her neck. His fingers suddenly gripped her throat and tightened.

"What were you looking for?" His voice was cold, grim.

Her breathing was cut off. Her eyes began to bulge. She tried to talk, managed only a wheeze.

Luke eased his grip. "What is it, Sadie?"

"Jeezus!" She pulled away from him, sank down on the edge of the bed, and began to massage her throat. "Is that any way to treat a lady?"

Ryatt grinned. "Some ladies."

She ran her tongue across her lips. They were moist, parted. It was a trick that came naturally to her, a defense mechanism. It usually worked with men.

"A pair of socks," she said. "That's what I was looking for. I told you I wanted to surprise you . . ."

She trailed off, watching him walk to the closet. Ryatt hunkered down beside his open Boston bag, picked up the telegram Coster had sent him. She must have been reading this when he walked in.

He looked back at her.

"A doxie named Sadie . . . she'd sell out her mother for two-bits."

96

Ryatt shoved the telegram into his pocket.

"You know more than you've told me," he said grimly. "You know why Ned went to the Corby place. And you know why Jeff was killed."

She shrank back as he walked back to her. "Jeezus — in the name of Mary Magdalene . . . I swear . . ."

He cut her off, his voice rough: "Don't, Sadie, they might hear you up there!"

She stared up at him, frightened now.

"All right, Sadie — what is out there? At Jeff's place?"

She shook her head. "I told you. I don't know anything. I don't know why Ned rode out there —"

He gripped her by the throat again, forced her back on the bed. *"Who killed Ned Coster?"*

She could breathe. She could just barely get through to talk. She wheezed: "As God is my witness, I don't know!"

Ryatt stood up, frowning.

Sadie remained on her back, shirttails up around her navel. She lay there, sobbing.

"Why don't you ask Amy Corby?" she cried. "If there's anything out there on her farm, ask her!"

Ryatt shrugged. "All right. Get dressed."

She didn't stir.

He reached out to pull her up — something on the dresser caught his attention. He went around the bed and picked it up. A small brown glass bottle, half full of liquid. He uncorked it and smelled it.

He turned, growling: "Laudanum." A solution of opium in alcohol. "What in hell are you using this stuff for?"

"I have . . . a cold . . ." She sniveled. "And . . . sometimes I get depressed . . ."

Ryatt shrugged. What the hell . . . half the whores in town were probably hooked on the stuff.

He said: "Come on. Let's get something to eat."

She didn't move. "I'm not hungry now."

"Suit yourself."

He walked to the door.

She turned toward him. "Don't go."

Ryatt waited.

"I waited all afternoon for you. I put on your shirt because I thought it would be different."

He walked back to the bed.

Her hands reached up, unbuttoning his shirt. "Luke . . . I get lonely . . ."

Ryatt felt the heat spread through his loins, the stiffening. Tomorrow he might be dead . . .

She helped him take his pants off. She sighed as he went into her.

"Oh, God. . . ."

The hotel dining room was more than half full and brightly lighted. Glasses clinked, plates clacked. Voices murmured in polite conversation.

The room had murals painted on the walls — buffalo herds grazing on endless, sunlit plains, a U.S. Cavalry unit on patrol, a railroad scene, blasting through a towering mountain pass . . .

Angus MacIntosh was there with a good-looking woman that Ryatt assumed was the Scotsman's wife. They were at a table with two other men, railroad officials. They looked up as Ryatt and Sadie walked by. Angus nodded greeting, but his wife turned her head away, made a stiff pretense of talking to one of the railroad men.

The same waiter served them. They sat away from the window this time. Sadie was subdued, her smile nervous. She was wearing a hat, and her dress was buttoned up to her neck.

The dinner menu featured buffalo steak, venison, and wild duck among other things. It had an extensive wine list.

Ryatt ordered, Sadie going with his choice.

"Champagne?" The waiter's eyebrows raised. He nodded. "Yes, sir."

Sadie looked across the table to Ryatt. She had never eaten in the Dodge House dining room before she met Ryatt. She knew she was not welcome here. Her kind stayed south of the deadline. They ate in the slop joints. They were lucky if they were still alive after thirty.

She said in a small voice: "What are we celebrating?"

Ryatt smiled. "You and I . . . a good meal . . ." He shrugged. "Tomorrow we might be dead."

Sadie shivered. "That . . . that's morbid."

"Practical," Ryatt answered.

The waiter came back with a three-legged iron stand and an ice bucket with a champagne bottle in it. French label. He popped the cork, poured. Heads turned. Eyes disapproved. Ryatt grinned. Hell with the bastards. It wasn't their lives on the line.

The waiter lingered. "Everything all right, sir?"

Ryatt nodded.

The waiter went away.

Sadie eyed the pale yellow, bubbling liquid in her glass.

"You like this stuff?"

"Grew up with it. My mother's ancestors were French. She said no gentleman would ever drink anything but champagne."

"Gee!" She picked up her glass and started to drink. The bubbles tickled her nose. She sneezed, spilling some down her sleeve.

She was embarrassed. "I'm sorry . . ."

Ryatt held up his glass. "Here's to us, Sadie. May there be no moaning at the bar, when we put out to sea . . ."

She didn't understand him.

"My apologies to Tennyson," Ryatt said.

"An English poet . . ." He smiled. "I went to a military college for a while."

She was quiet for a long moment, staring into her glass, then: "I was kicked out of the third grade. Small town in Iowa. Didn't matter much. My father was the town drunk."

"You do pretty well with the English language."

She brightened a little. "School ain't the only place to get an education," she said.

"Guess not."

She leaned toward him. "You know, from the way Ned talked, I pictured you different. Kinda like . . . like those Texans coming up the trail, bustling into places like the Lady Gay with only one thing in mind." She signed. "You know what I mean."

"I went to school in Virginia," Ryatt said. He turned his glass around between his palms, staring down into the champagne. He wasn't usually reflective, and he was seldom talkative . . . but he felt like talking tonight.

"Went to a military academy. My father came from Virginia, a small town south of Roanoke. My mother, too." He shrugged. "I never knew why they came west to settle in West Texas . . ."

"Dead?"

He nodded. "Like a lot of things."

He reached for the bottle and refilled her glass.

"You ashamed of me?" Her voice was barely audible.

He looked at her. "No."

"I never had champagne before. I don't know as I like it." Her eyes searched Ryatt's face. "And I —"

"You're a woman," he cut in quietly. "And you're good at what you do."

She smiled. "I am?"

He raised his glass. "Come on, Sadie. Let's drink to —"

The window to their right blew inward as a Sharp buffalo gun smashed through the panes. The heavy slug ripped through one of the murals on the back wall, smashed into a heavy iron pot in the kitchen, and ricocheted into one of the cooks, knocking him against a long table.

Men and women dove for the safety of the floor as the second slug smashed into one of the ceiling chandeliers, showering glass over the tables.

Silence fell.

Then a man's voice sounded, loud and clear and ugly. "Come on out, Marshal! We're waiting for you!"

Rego Larsen had come back!

102

12

Ryatt was on the floor, by the table. He reached out and touched Sadie's hand. She was huddled next to him, pale-faced, frightened.

"Stay down!" he told her. "Don't move!"

One more shot smashed through the already shattered window. Then Rego's voice:

"Marshal!"

Ryatt raised his voice: "Hold your fire, Rego! I'm coming out!"

Rego's voice answered, an impatience riding it, a sneer: "I'm giving you one minute, Marshal! Then we come in after you!"

Ryatt backed away from Sadie, got to his feet, and ran past Angus MacIntosh's table, toward the lobby. He had left his guns in his room.

There were people on the stairs, frightened, asking questions. Ryatt shouldered past them, took the stairs two at a time, and ducked into his room. He found his cartridge belts, strapped them around his lean waist, and checked the loads. He went to the closet and hauled out his Boston bag.

He didn't know how many of Rego's friends were out there, where they were. And it was night. A man could miss in the dark with a Colt, even at close quarters. A shadow moving, that would be all he'd see . . . all the time he'd have.

He found what he was after in the bottom of the bag. One of the tools of his trade. A double-barreled shotgun, sawed off to fourteen inches all told. Nicely balanced. Not much good at a distance . . . made a hell of a mess at close quarters.

It had a leather sling for easy carry.

Ryatt snugged two shells into the twin chambers. Buckshot. He stuffed extra shells into his coat pocket, checked his belly gun. He might need them all.

He had left a lamp burning, turned low . . . he didn't touch it. He didn't want to give anyone watching something to consider. They were out front, and quite likely someone was posted in back of the hotel, but they couldn't know the location of his room.

Ryatt crossed to the window, slinging his cut-down shotgun over his right shoulder. He eased the sash up carefully, an inch at a time. It was quiet outside in the street. It was very quiet inside the hotel.

He flattened against the wall by the window and looked out. An alley separated him from the flat roof of an adjoining building. Eight feet wide, it looked like, and a floor below him.

Ryatt considered his chances. A sliver of moon rode low in the west; it didn't throw much light. High riding clouds dimmed the stars . . .

A cool wind blew against the lace curtains. Ryatt leaned out and studied the cornice around the window. The bottom part made a small ledge, about four inches wide. Wide enough for him to stand on.

He hooked a leg over the sill, eased his foot down until his booted toe found the ledge. He tested it. It seemed firm enough.

He slid his other foot across the sill, eased out, and balanced himself on the narrow cornice. He knew he was a sitting duck, if someone was in the alley, watching. He didn't wait to find out.

He jumped. He cleared the alley easily enough and landed on the flat roof of the building beyond. He felt the tar-papered, weathered boards crack under his weight and had the sudden sickening feeling he was going through. But the roof held, and he fell forward on his hands and knees, his slung shotgun banging against his elbow.

Someone moved in the hotel's backyard.

Ryatt crawled to the edge of the roof and looked down. The hotel stable was a huge, dark blotch in a pooling darkness. Inside, horses stamped uneasily.

Ryatt waited. Someone was down there . . . someone who was watching the hotel's back door. He couldn't see him, but he sensed him.

Ryatt waited.

From out in the street Rego's voice lifted: "Yaegar . . . Bodreau . . . I'm going in after the bastid!"

A shadow moved against the bulking stables. The man paused, looked down the alley, and hesitated. That was as far as he was going to go.

Ryatt had to chance it. He eased his body over the edge, fingers hooking, holding. He let go, dropped silently, falling five or six feet. One foot came down on a tin can; he stumbled, whirled, the shotgun coming up in his hands . . .

The man waiting by the stable wall heard him. Wasn't sure. He stepped out away from the building. Dim light showed Ryatt a long-shanked man, fringed buckskin jacket, a strip of red calico cloth around his forehead, holding back black, greasy hair . . .

Ryatt stepped away from the building. The man spun around and fired. The heavy slug whistled past Ryatt, ripping into the warped boards of the flat roofed building.

Ryatt blew the ambusher back against the stables with a load of buckshot, spun away as the man fell, and went running down the alley, out into the street.

Out on Front Street someone yelled: "Yaegar . . . what happened, Yaegar . . . ?"

He was across from the Dodge House, covering the hotel's entrance. He came running now toward the alley, a rifle in his hands.

He spotted Ryatt coming out of the darkness, skidded to a stop, and got off a wild shot.

Ryatt closed to within fifteen feet of the buffalo hunter. The man yelled: "Rego! Out here, Rego . . ." as he dropped the rifle and reached for his skinning knife.

Ryatt's shotgun blasted him back. He fell like a rag doll, the stuffing spilling out of it.

Rego Larsen came running out of the hotel. He saw Ryatt in the middle of the street, crouched over Bodreau's unmoving body.

A curse welled up in the wild buffalo hunter's throat, anger tearing at him. He steadied himself against the porch support at the head of the stairs and levelled his big Sharps rifle.

Ryatt saw him. He dropped the empty shotgun and drew his Colt. It was a long shot for a handgun, and he didn't expect a hit. He didn't even try.

Rego Larsen was braced against the support, sweating, sighting toward the figure out in the street. He had one shot in the buffalo gun; he had to make it good.

Ryatt spoiled it.

He emptied his Colt at Rego, the bullets splintering the porch support, driving Rego back. The buffalo gun roared, the heavy slug missing Ryatt by a foot. Rego stumbled, fell to one knee, and dropped his rifle.

He was reaching for his sheath knife when Ryatt came running up. He looked into Ryatt's levelled Colt, his hand tightening on the knife handle . . .

"Don't make me kill you!" Ryatt's voice was flat, deadly.

The buffalo hunter was crouched down. He stood still, undecided. Ryatt reached for the knife, took it from Rego and tossed it away.

The fight went out of the man then. He said bitterly: "Yaegar . . . Bodreau . . . ?"

"Took a load of buckshot," Ryatt answered him. "Maybe they'll live. They won't be hunting buffalo."

Rego Larsen's breath smell of raw, busting whiskey. Must have tanked up before coming to town, Ryatt thought.

The buffalo hunter sat down on the porch steps, a sigh gusting out of him. "God-dam . . ." he said, putting his face between his hands. "Goddam . . ."

Slowly, cautiously, people came out of the Dodge House, pausing in the doorway, crowding onto the wide, covered porch. Staring, whispering. Down the street other people clustered and watched.

The man called Bodreau stirred, groaned.

He started to drag himself toward the hotel.

Someone behind Ryatt said: "Fetch Doctor Hayden! That one's still alive."

Fred Gelson detached himself from the group down the street and came striding toward the hotel. Angus pushed his way through the people crowding the hotel entrance and stopped by Ryatt.

"There's another one in back," Ryatt told him. "Down by the stable."

Angus turned to men behind him. "Get those wounded men inside, in the lobby. Doctor Hayden can take care of them there."

Ryatt hauled Rego to his feet. Fred Gelson was just coming up the stairs. Ryatt turned to him. "Kelly mentioned a jailer — a man by the name of Olaf . . ."

Gelson nodded.

"Get him."

Angus said: "You all right, Luke?"

Ryatt saw the concern in the Scotsman's face, knew it was genuine.

"I was lucky," he said.

He pushed the buffalo hunter down the steps ahead of him. Some men had picked up Bodreau. They were carrying the wounded man into the hotel.

Ryatt stopped to pick up his shotgun. A switch engine puffed by, heading for the rail yards beyond. The engineer stared curiously from his cab; he did not know what had happened.

Ryatt walked Rego down the street to the law office. The buffalo hunter kept his head down. The whiskey was getting to him. He staggered as he walked.

Ryatt opened the door, lighted a lamp, shoved Rego inside one of the cells, and locked it. The buffalo hunter sat on the edge of his bunk, head in his hands.

Ryatt was sprawled in a chair by the desk, smoking a cigar, when Fred Gelson showed up behind a big, shambling, boney-faced man.

Ryatt said: "Olaf?"

"Yah."

"We've got a prisoner."

Olaf walked to the cell, looked in on Rego Larsen, and came back.

"I don't think he has any more friends," Ryatt said. "Not in town anyway." He stood up and found his hat. "Let me know if he tries to give you any trouble."

The Swede rubbed his big-knuckled hands together. "Yah . . ." He turned to look at the prisoner. "No trouble, Marshal."

Fred Gelson walked outside with Ryatt. They paused on the walk, Fred lighting a ready-made cigarette.

"Wicked looking weapon," the news-paperman said. He was referring to the cut-down shotgun slung across Ryatt's shoulder. "Only saw one other like it. Gambler by the name of Sweeney. Got caught cheating in a poker game, had a knife blade drived through his right hand. Happened on a Mississippi riverboat. The Natchez Queen, I think. Sweeney didn't say a word. He got up, wrapped his handkerchief around his hand, and went back to his stateroom. Couple of minutes later he returned with a shotgun like that, blew the other guy apart."

"I knew Sweeney," Ryatt said. His cigar tasted good. The town was quiet.

"Got this gun from him. Won it in a poker game. Same riverboat . . ."

Gelson shook his head. "You were lucky tonight, Luke. Those buffalo hunters were liquored up, careless." He looked past Ryatt, toward the deadline.

"You'll need more than luck riding with you tomorrow."

Ryatt grinned. "Gambler's odds. Double or nothing?"

Gelson stared at him.

"Thirty thousand if I make it back and check in?"

Gelson exploded: "You're crazy!"

He started to walk away but suddenly turned. "The paper comes out Friday. I'm still keeping that obit in type."

Ryatt shrugged. "Save me a copy."

13

Ned Costner's widow stirred in bed, sighing. She turned to snuggle closer to warmth, her hand reaching out for Ryatt. She awakened then, still sleep-drugged, aware she was alone in bed. Fear made a cold, hard knot in her stomach.

Gray morning seeped through the glass panes like early ground fog. The sun's rays were low, slanting in from across the river. They had not yet reached into the hotel bedroom.

Ryatt was dressed. New white shirt, string tie, long black coat. She noticed he had shaved. The faint odor of talcum powder lingered.

A pang of jealousy shot through her. She sat up. "Luke . . . ?"

He turned to her, a smile in his glance, reassuring her.

"Where are you going?"

"Make the rounds."

"So early?" There was a plaintive note in her voice. "It's barely daylight."

Ryatt shrugged and strapped on his guns.

"Wait!" The laudanum still drugged her reactions. "Wait for me, Luke. I'll have breakfast with you."

"No need."

She studied him, fear returning. An emptiness. She had slept with many men since turning fifteen. Why should this one be different? But watching Ryatt, she felt something stir inside her . . . something at once sad and bitter . . . a fleeting regret for what might have been, had she turned out different or met Ryatt earlier.

"Please? I want to come with you."

"No. I'm just having coffee this morning."

She got out of bed anyway. She liked to sleep nude when it was warm enough; she had nothing on now. She didn't mind. She had long ago gotten over feeling embarrassment at the look in men's eyes. Hers was still a firm, rounded figure . . . nothing to be ashamed of.

"Luke . . . last night . . . I was afraid . . ."

He shrugged. "So was I."

She came up close to him, shivering . . . it wasn't the early morning chill.

"Not like that. I wasn't afraid of those men, Luke. I was afraid for you . . . afraid you might not come back to me."

Ryatt walked to the bed, pulled the coverlet off, and draped it around Sadie's shoulders.

She looked up into Ryatt's hard face, a question in her eyes.

"I like to keep my mind on my work," Ryatt said quietly. "I can't, if you —"

She shrugged the coverlet off and hugged him, pressing her body against him.

"Luke, take me with you when you leave?"

"Maybe." It was thinking too far ahead. There was the day to get through — and the night. The Colonel was waiting for him in the Lady Gay.

She shivered again.

"I liked the champagne, Luke — I really did. And I can learn —"

He led her back to the bed, tucked her in.

"We'll celebrate tonight," he said. "If I get back."

She looked up into his face, her voice catching in her throat.

"If you get back?"

He chucked her under the chin and smiled. "I'll be back. That's a promise."

She watched him leave, her thoughts in turmoil. After a while she got up, walked to the dresser, and studied herself in the mirror. The lines of her body were still good, her breasts still firm. But her hips were beginning to thicken, her buttocks beginning to sag.

She didn't try fooling herself. Her body was all she had to offer. And one day it would all sag. One day she'd be old and wrinkled, and then she'd be old and alone.

She backed off, her eyes dark, tortured —

the old gray depression was coming over her.

She turned toward the door. "Luke," she whispered, "take me with you. Please . . . ?"

But she knew he wouldn't.

She went back to the dresser and picked up the bottle of laudanum. She needed it. It eased the pain, brightened the days, and made her forget what she was.

She took the bottle to bed with her.

The sun was still low on the horizon when Ryatt walked into the Dodge House dining room. The morning was crisp, clear. A wagon drove down Front Street, the wheels churning up small patches of mud.

Ryatt sat at a table and watched the men work on the windows, replacing the broken glass. He drank coffee and glanced over an old copy of the St. Louis Dispatch, which had been brought in and left by some past traveler. President Grant was being accused of malfeasance in office . . .

Angus came down into the lobby and turned into the dining room. He spotted Ryatt and crossed the room to join him, sliding a chair out from under the table.

"You're up early," Angus said.

"Habit." Ryatt drew his legs under him and laid the newspaper aside. "You?"

"Grew up on a farm," Angus replied. "Up with the sun. Still do."

The waiter came up with more coffee. He

refilled Ryatt's cup and poured some for Angus.

"Biscuits and marmalade," Angus ordered. "Wouldn't mind kippers once in a while," he said as the waiter moved away, "but the damn fools here don't even know what kippers are."

"A shame," Ryatt said. He was wondering why Angus was here.

The Scotsman sipped his coffee. "My wife's still in bed," he said abruptly. It seemed to him to be the best way to start it. "She's a city girl . . . born in Baltimore."

Ryatt smiled faintly. "There's a difference?"

"About last night," Angus began stiffly. "When you and that girl came by our table —"

"I understand."

"Do you?" Angus looked uncomfortable. "Hell, I don't give a damn whom you consort with, Marshal. But my wife —"

"Doesn't like it." Ryatt grinned over the rim of his coffee cup. "Forget it, Angus."

"No." There was a stubbornness in Angus' eyes. "Loretta avoids Kelly for the same reason. She knows about his housekeeper —"

He paused as the waiter came up with his biscuits and a small jar of English marmalade.

"I just wanted you to know," he muttered.

Ryatt shrugged. "It didn't bother me, Angus. I don't live here. I expect to be leaving soon. And your wife has a right to be choosing the company she keeps."

Angus nodded. "That's the other thing I wanted to talk to you about, Luke."

"My leaving?"

"The Colonel. Fred tells me you're going after him tonight?"

Ryatt leaned back in his chair. "Isn't that what the city is paying me for?"

Angus shook his head. "No. Not me anyway. The Colonel is really Morry's problem. If he had paid those Texans what they had coming for their trail here —"

Ryatt cut him short. "Morry didn't. And the law says he doesn't have to."

"Yes, I know." Angus looked around the dining room. A workman was examining the damage done to the back wall. There were only a few other early diners in the room. None of them were women.

"You notice how little traffic we've got coming into town, Marshal?"

Ryatt nodded. "It does seem kind of slow."

"Since Abilene shut them off, we were getting most of the Texas beef coming up the trail. Wasn't a week we didn't have longhorns bedding down across the river. Texas drovers coming into town, laying the whores, playing the tiger, drinking up the rotgut. Most of them confined their celebration to the joints south of the deadline. They shot up a few bars, landed in jail. They left in the morning,

117

busted, heads aching, but happy. Most of them, anyway."

"What happened?"

"It stopped right after the Colonel arrived here with his herd. He took Morry's money all right — I guess he had to. Morry figured they'd leave . . . we hoped they would."

Angus shrugged. "We knew we had big trouble when the Colonel took over the Lady Gay. Paid the owner, Wall-eye Jensen, ten cents on the dollar for the place. Made it stick. He ran out the whores and settled in. The past couple of weeks they've been meeting the herds down the trail, warning them about Morry's prices. Most of them believed him. Those who didn't were turned away at the point of a gun. Some of that Texas beef has swung back to Abilene, the others heading for the mining camps around Denver."

"I can see why the town wants the Colonel and his men out," Ryatt said.

"Morry Teague most of all," Angus muttered. "He's the biggest cattle buyer in the area. Buys beef for the Western Beef Packing Company, offices in Chicago. He buys trail-toughened longhorns, fattens them in his feed lots and then ships them east by rail. Over a quarter of a million head this year alone . . ."

Ryatt leaned across the table, eyes narrowing, something occurring to him.

"Morry must handle a lot of money?"

"I would imagine so." Angus scowled. "Morry keeps his business to himself. Doesn't even trust the bank. Keeps his money in a safe in his office."

"Seems ripe for a holdup," Ryatt observed.

"Oh, it was tried," Angus said. "Someone blew his office safe open just a few weeks ago. About the time the Colonel took over the Lady Gay."

"How much did Morry lose?"

"Nothing." Angus shrugged. "Morry never made any fuss over it. He said he was lucky — nothing in the safe that day except some invoices and a few cancelled checks . . ."

"No money at all, eh?" There was skepticism in Ryatt's tone.

"Hell," Angus muttered, "if Morry had lost money he wouldn't have hidden it. Not Morry. He would have made a big stink about it. But the money doesn't belong to him, anyway. It's the meat packing company's money. He remits by railroad express once a month."

A little black ball was bouncing around in the roulette wheel inside Ryatt's head, waiting to drop into one of the slots.

He said: "Where's Morry now?"

"I just saw him ride out of town," Angus replied. "Said he was joining his men rounding up the beef he lost the other night."

He paused as he spotted his wife coming into the dining room.

He stood up, saying: "Look, Marshal . . . if you need help tonight —"

"I don't," Ryatt said evenly. "But thanks, anyway."

He watched the Scotsman join his wife. She was staring toward Ryatt with cold disapproval, and she said something in a sharp voice to Angus as he came up.

Ryatt saw Angus's back stiffen and heard his voice carry: "No! It's none of your business, Loretta!" She started to say something to this but he cut her off, taking her arm and marching her out of the dining room.

Ryatt finished his coffee, signed his tab, and walked out of the hotel.

The sun had climbed higher, and the puddles in the street were drying. Shops were opening, and people were going about their business. The sound of a blacksmith's hammer rang on the still air.

It was, Ryatt thought, a nice time to buy a farm.

14

Amy Corby's sister, Rena, was a sharp-faced, angular woman, very unlike Jeff Corby's widow. It was hard for Ryatt to believe they were sisters.

She had answered the door. Now she stared at him, frowning her disapproval. "I'm sorry, Marshal. But Amy's busy packing —"

"She leaving?"

"Tomorrow. Going back to St. Louis."

Ryatt ran this through his mind. "I talked to her yesterday. She told me she was waiting to sell the farm —"

"She did. Last night." Rena's tone was sharp. "Now if you'll excuse me —"

She turned to go back inside the house. Ryatt put his foot in the doorway.

"I'd like to speak to her anyway."

"Why?" Amy's sister's voice was unfriendly. "I don't see that it's any of your business —"

The man coming down the hallway behind her cut in heavily: "Who is it, Rena?"

He was a stoop-shouldered, rawboned man, suspenders pulled up over a gray woolen shirt. He looked much older than Rena.

Grayshot whiskers hid a thin-lipped mouth.

He looked over her shoulder at Ryatt, saw the badge, and softened his tone:

"What is it, Marshal?"

"I'd like to speak to Mrs. Corby."

The man hesitated.

His wife said: "You know she doesn't want to see anyone, Will."

"Why don't you ask her?" Ryatt said bluntly. "She'll talk to me. Just tell her I know why Jeff went to the Lady Gay that night . . ."

Rena's eyes narrowed. "I think that's in poor taste, Marshal —"

Ryatt shrugged. "Then let's just say I know what's at the farm. She'll understand."

The man looked puzzled; so did his wife. He rubbed his hands together and muttered: "Go ahead, Rena — tell her. Maybe she will see the Marshal."

He stood blocking the doorway, not asking Ryatt inside. He was not an outgoing man. He watched Ryatt, ill at ease with himself, his hands digging into his pockets.

After a few moments Amy Corby appeared, walking ahead of her sister.

She said coldly: "Just what is it you want, Mr. Ryatt?"

"A chance to bid on your farm."

She shook her head. "I'm sure my sister has already informed you the farm's been sold."

"To whom?"

She looked at him, weighing his question, then said: "To Morry Teague."

It figured. The little black roulette ball bouncing around in his head fell into its slot.

"I'm sorry you sold out so hastily, Mrs. Corby," he said. "I came prepared to double whatever anyone offered you for it."

She frowned. She was still dressed in black, but even in black she didn't look drab, not like her sister Rena. There was a cool sparkle in her eyes.

"Why? Why do you want to buy the farm?"

"Because I know what's out there," he said.

For an instant something flickered inside her cool gray eyes — something unsettling that masked almost immediately.

She sighed. "Well, if you do it's more than I know. We made a living off the farm, that's about all." She shrugged. "Anyway, I'm truly sorry, Mr. Ryatt. I know you were a friend of Jeff's. But I have already signed papers, accepted Mr. Teague's money . . ."

"Too bad," Ryatt said.

He put his hat back on his head. "It appears to me you sold out cheap, Mrs. Corby."

Her eyes narrowed now, anger peering out. "Maybe you should tell me, Marshal. Just what is supposed to be buried out there on the farm I don't know about —"

"Did I say buried?"

She bit her lip. "Whatever!" Her voice was

cold. "Just what are you getting at?"

"I'll let you know tomorrow," Ryatt said. "If you're still here."

He swung away from the door, walking down the garden walk. He could feel her gaze on his back, sharp and penetrating. She was disturbed. He chuckled to himself. That was the way he wanted it.

The Dodge City stables were at the far end of town, up by the first of Morry Teague's feedlots. They had horses for hire.

A pile of fresh manure steamed in a corner of the trampled yard. Flies buzzed busily. The stableman set his pitchfork aside as Ryatt walked to the corral and looked inside.

"Big Blackie there's the best we got, Marshal," the stableman said; pointing. He had a big, freshly cut chaw of tobacco bulging against a grizzled cheek.

"You're a liar," Ryatt said, the tone of his voice carrying no offense. "No bottom. Run him hard, and he'll quit on you."

The stableman aimed a stream of tobacco juice at the manure pile. "Take your pick," he said surlily. "Three dollars a day —"

There were six horses inside the corral. "The roan," Ryatt said, pointing. "Not as big as the black, maybe got a mean streak in him, too."

The stableman shrugged. "Guess you know your horses," he said. "Ain't been ridden in a week. That mean streak's just friskiness."

"Saddle him."

He waited while the stableman went into the corral with a hackamore, cornered the roan, slipped it over his head, and led him outside.

Ryatt had ridden better horses. But this one would do. He didn't expect to get into any trouble riding out to Jeff Corby's place. All he wanted was a look around. He figured he'd have that much time to kill. He didn't expect to find what he knew was hidden out there. That could come later.

The saddle the stableman slapped on the roan was old, but Ryatt settled into it comfortably. The roan danced under him, feeling him out. Ryatt kept a firm hand on the reins, saying: "I'll let you run, boy — soon as we get out of town!"

Henry Oliver was waiting in front of the law office as Ryatt rode by. He yelled something to the marshal and waved a paper at him.

Ryatt figured it was a court injunction. He ignored it.

They watched him ride by the Lady Gay on his way south, heading toward the river. The Colonel and the big man called Rafe.

The burly man said: "Looks to me like he's leaving town."

The Colonel shook his head. "He'll be back."

"Where's he going then?"

The Colonel shrugged. "Let's find out. Take Barney with you."

Rafe scowled. "Could be he's heading for Jeff Corby's place."

"Maybe."

Rafe knuckled his unshaven chin. "You figure he knows?"

"I wouldn't be surprised," the Colonel said. "Ned Coster asked him to come."

He put a hand on Rafe's arm as the big man turned to go. "Find out where he's going. Don't try to stop him . . . don't let him see you. I want you and Barney back here before sundown!"

He waited until Rafe and Barney saddled up and rode out. The others watched him, waiting for orders.

It was mid-morning and the sun was beginning to heat up. It would be hot again by nightfall.

Barney was just a kid, but he didn't trust Rafe. The big man was getting restive. In the army he'd be the kind who would be doing time in the stockade. He was big, and he was dangerous, but he wasn't smart. And that would mean his life some day.

Maybe he had sent the wrong men after Ryatt. He shrugged.

Ryatt would be back. Somehow he was sure of that. He wasn't so sure about Rafe and Barney.

15

Ryatt followed the Arkansas northeast for a few miles, then cut across rolling prairie country, heading for Walnut Creek, which came down from the north to meet the bigger river.

He let the roan run, the wind in his face still morning cool. The Arkansas ran wide, still swollen from the recent rain. He cut across the rails of the Santa Fe, following the river, heading back to Abilene and Hays City, all the way back to St. Louis. He was in Indian territory, Cheyenne and Kiowa country. They were raiding further south now, pushed back from the river by soldiers from Fort Dodge and Fort Larned and by cavalry patrols protecting the railroad.

Buffalo wallows were everywhere. But the big buffalo herds were gone, hunted out by the professional buffalo hunters and by parties who came west by Santa Fe railroad and shot them from the windows of their sleeping-cars for sport. There were still large herds roaming further south, but Ryatt knew they, too, would soon become a thing of the past.

A short while later Ryatt came across the Western Trail, that branch of the Chisum that started in Texas and had been feeding more than a million steers into Dodge. For miles around the prairie grass was trampled, the ground bare, lifeless. The rain had turned the wallows into mudholes, the trampled areas into quagmires. Ryatt skirted them, heading toward Little Coon Creek where he had been told Jeff's farm was located.

Somewhere along the way he had the feeling he was being followed. He topped a rise, looked back, and found his suspicions justified.

The two riders turned northeast, riding away from him. They were too far for him to make out.

Ryatt waited until they had dipped down out of sight. Could be he was wrong. Maybe they were just a couple of travelers, heading for the crossing on the Arkansas.

The early morning run had taken the skittishness out of the roan, he settled down now to an easy, ground-eating gait. Ryatt spotted a burned-out wagon in a gully, the victim of some past Indian attack. Farther on he came across a sod hut that had been abandoned; the people who had built it and lived in it had either been frightened off or had just plain given up.

The land grew rougher now with gullies and thickets breaking the run of the prairie.

A few miles beyond the sod hut he saw the first of Morry Teague's scattered beef. The roan-colored steer had been shot and left lying on the prairie, the ravens and crows already feeding on the carcasses.

Ryatt dismounted to examine the brand. A "Circle M" had been burned into the hide, and a smaller "MT" burned into the shoulder. The Colonel's beef, with Morry Teague's brand on the shoulder.

Ryatt had seen no sign of Morry or the men working for him, but someone else had been out here after the stampede . . . someone taking pleasure in shooting Morry's beef. Ryatt knuckled his chin. It wasn't hard to figure out who.

Riding on, he spotted several other carcasses before topping a low rise that dropped down to a wide gully. Two of Morry's men were working this area. There was a chuck wagon about two hundred yards below Ryatt, and a makeshift brush corral just beyond with maybe thirty bawling steers inside.

The two men were hunkered down around a late breakfast, the smoke curling up in a thin blue banner. They spotted Ryatt as he topped the rise, and the taller man whirled, grabbed his rifle propped up against the side of the wagon, and fired a quick shot.

The bullet snarled past Ryatt, missing him by less than a foot. The roan reared. Ryatt fought the animal, bringing him back under control.

He raised both hands high and yelled: "Hold your fire!"

The man who had fired the shot was already working the lever of his carbine. He jerked the muzzle up as he pulled the trigger, the shot going high now, the whipcrack sound fading.

The paunchy, older man behind him said: "Go take a look, Johnson . . . I'll cover you."

Ryatt watched him come up the slope. The man behind Johnson stood by the wagon, his rifle ready. Ryatt knew why they were skittish and didn't blame them.

Ryatt waited until Johnson was only a few feet away before asking: "You work for Morry Teague?"

Johnson nodded, his pale gray eyes wary. He was a rangy man in work Levis, flannel shirt, and a brush jacket. The lines in his face were deep, but he was still a young man. He wasn't wearing a gun belt.

He eyed Ryatt's badge, relaxed. "Sorry, Marshal," he said. "We weren't expecting you."

Ryatt looked past him, to the wagon. "Morry down there?"

Johnson shook his head. "Haven't seen Mr. Teague." He waved to the man by the wagon. "Me and Resko have been out here since yesterday morning, rounding up Morry's beef."

He shrugged. "You looking for Morry Teague?"

Ryatt said: "No . . . just looking around." He went with Johnson down the slope to the wagon. "Saw some steers branded 'Circle M' and 'MT' shot a ways back."

Johnson nodded grimly. "There's more, Marshal." He swung around to Resko coming away from the wagon, still holding his rifle. "It's all right, Resko . . . it's the new town marshal —"

He paused, looking askance at Luke.

"Luke Ryatt," Luke said. "Picked up the badge two days ago." From the way these men acted it looked like Morry Teague had not told them about him.

Resko nodded. "Howdy, Marshal." He was wearing cheap town clothes, muddied and ill-fitting. Range work was not what he was hired for, evidently.

"Some bastard's been shooting our steers," he went on. "We figgered you might be one of them when you topped that ridge."

Ryatt said: "You haven't seen Morry?"

Resko frowned. "He out here?"

"Left town this morning to join you," Ryatt replied.

Johnson looked at Resko. "Could be he ran into Hamby and Jones first. They're farther north, combing the river breaks."

Ryatt didn't think so, but he kept this to himself. He swung out of his saddle and tied the roan to the wagon wheel.

Johnson said: "We were raided the other night. Steers stampeded out of Mr. Teague's holding pens and scattered all over hell. I guess Mr. Teague told you about it."

Ryatt nodded. "He did."

"That sonuvabitch Texan that calls himself the Colonel," Resko said harshly. "That's the man you want, Marshal." He scrubbed his unshaven cheek and spat. "Sonuvabitch's crazy —"

Ryatt said: "I'll take care of him." His tone was matter-of-fact. He looked toward the campfire. "Any coffee left?"

"A whole potful," Johnson answered. "Was just setting down to eat when yuh showed up."

Ryatt joined them around the fire. Resko found an extra cup and filled it with strong, black brew. "Biscuits and beans," he said, "You're welcome, Marshal."

The ride had given an edge to Ryatt's appetite. He nodded and dug in with them.

"Hell of a job rounding up these goddam Texas steers," Johnson said, his mouth full. "Skittish as a pregnant coyote and twice as ornery."

"Not my kind of job," Resko said. "Wouldn't be out here if Morry hadn't promised me double wages." He brushed his sleeve across his lip. "Beats hell what a man with a wife and kids will do for money —"

Ryatt agreed. He finished his coffee, stood up, and asked directions to Jeff's farm.

"The Corby place?" Johnson looked at Resko who seemed to know. "Sure," the paunchy man said. "Due east of here, about six, seven miles. Can't miss it. Only farm on Coon Creek."

Ryatt went to his horse, untied it, and mounted. They didn't know about Morry buying the Corby farm; they were just hired hands.

He said: "Thanks for the beans and coffee. If I see Morry, I'll tell him where you are."

From the far side of the gully Rafe and Barney watched Ryatt ride away. They had circled after being spotted by the marshal, coming back this way and finding cover across the gully under shale rock. The Johnson-Resko camp was a good three hundred and fifty yards away — a long shot for a .30-30 Winchester.

Rafe licked his lips. He waited until Ryatt was gone before saying: "Think you can get the paunchy one, Barney?"

Barney was toting a Sharps .54-40. It had the range. In good hands it could kill at twice the distance.

Barney said: "Sure. No trouble at all."

Rafe wiped his nose with the back of his hand. "Those are our cows," he said. "They owe us . . ."

Barney looked at him. "We'll lose Ryatt."

Rafe shrugged. "Don't matter. I know where he's headed."

"The Corby place?"

"Where else." He flattened down and shoved his Winchester muzzle up ahead of him.

Barney hesitated. "The Colonel won't like it, Rafe. Us killing them."

"Hell with the Colonel!" Rafe snarled. "I've about had it with him. If I had my way —"

Below them Resko had come away from the fire. He was looking across the gully toward them. Maybe he had spotted something. He began to walk toward his rifle propped against the wagon wheel.

Rafe said sharply: "All right, get him, Barney!"

Barney's big Sharps boomed, the heavy slug hitting Resko high, knocking him back against the wagon. The paunchy man fell to his knees, eyes shocked with pain, blood pumping from the ugly bullet hole in his back. Barely conscious, he started to crawl toward his rifle.

Johnson made a run for his rifle, scooped it up and rolled under the wagon as Rafe's two quick shots missed by inches.

Rafe swore. Barney had reloaded the single-shot Sharps; he took dead aim and killed Resko as the man reached up for his rifle.

"Cover me," Rafe snarled. He stood up

and started to run down the steep slope toward the wagon. He tripped, fell headlong, and rolled. He managed to hold onto his rifle as he scrambled to his feet.

Johnson's slug whined off a rock inches from his face. Barney's Sharps boomed, driving Johnson back under the wagon. Rafe kept running toward camp. Johnson saw him at the last moment. He rolled away, to the far side of the wagon, and made a break for cover.

Barney had him covered all the way. The heavy Sharps slug smashed into his back between the shoulder blades. Johnson was dead before he hit the ground.

Rafe came running up, rifle ready. He saw that Johnson was dead and waved to Barney. Inside the brush enclosure steers were bawling, setting up a nerve-jangling clamor.

Barney went back for the picketed horses, mounted his, and rode down to join Rafe, leading Rafe's mean-eyed sorrel.

Barney looked around. Smoke still curled up from the dying fire. The wagon horses were picketed a few yards away, along with Johnson's saddle horse. Johnson had done most of the rounding up of the scattered steers while Resko tended camp.

"Think he heard us?"

Rafe said: "The Marshal?" He shook his head. "None of his business, anyway."

He reloaded his Winchester and walked to

the brush corral. "Eight dollars a head, Barney. That's all Morry Teague said they were worth."

There were thirty steers inside that enclosure; they killed them all.

For good measure they killed the horses and set fire to the wagon. Smoke was billowing up into the cloudless sky as they rode away, heading for Corby's place on Coon Creek.

16

The Colonel had his breakfast brought in to the Lady Gay from the lunchroom down the street. He always ate alone, sitting by the window, a quiet, fastidious man clinging to outmoded ideals.

In the Army an officer never ate with enlisted men. But the war was over. There was no longer a Confederate Army, nor a South as he remembered it. And he had never been a Colonel. It didn't matter. The men who had come up the Trail with him were Texans, some of them hard-scrabble cattlemen. Like him they had straggled back for a lost war, trying to pick up the pieces of their lives. They had gone back to farms, to small ranches, pooling their half-wild longhorns, coming up the long trail to Dodge with him. Putting everything they owned on the line, on the booming market in Dodge, only to be robbed by a sharp-dealing Yankee cattle buyer!

Maybe!

The Colonel ate his eggs and bacon and drank his coffee. All around him were momentoes of what this place had been — a house of ill repute. An oil painting of a naked woman hung behind the bar and there were red curtains in the upstairs rooms. He had not changed anything. But it pained him to be living here. An officer and a gentleman . . .

He finished his breakfast and went upstairs to his room. He wasn't a blue-nosed Puritan, but he had his scruples. For him there were only two kinds of women, the good and the bad, and he drew the line sharply between them.

He put on his gray tunic, brushed his grayshot hair, and set his cap squarely on his head. It was his campaign hat, banded and still spotless. He checked the gun he carried in his shoulder holster. It was oiled, ready.

There was a lot at stake. More than his pride. There was money on the line — more than enough money to give them all a fresh start.

He picked up his polished mahogany swagger stick, tucked it under his left arm, and drew on white gloves.

A good military tactician learned to plan his moves in advance, and he had to figure out all the angles. Ryatt would be coming back; somehow the Colonel was sure of this. And Ryatt knew where the money was!

Because Ned Coster's whore had told him!

There were five men left inside the Lady

Gay. They took their turn behind the bar. One of them was back there now, cleaning up. The other four were cleaning their guns, oiling them. They watched the Colonel come down the stairs and go out. They didn't say anything. They were used to the Colonel's strange ways.

The Colonel walked up the street, the morning sun at his back. He walked with a long, stiff-legged stride, shoulders squared, eyes cold under the brim of his hat.

The bars and whorehouses south of the deadline were closed. But girls watched him from upper-floor windows. The word had gone out about the coming showdown in the Lady Gay. The whores, the gamblers, and the bar owners were on the Colonel's side, although none of them liked him. Tomorrow they hoped to be in full swing again. Tomorrow they would be looking forward to burying another goddam town marshal!

The Colonel crossed the deadline. This was the respectable side of Dodge, this was where the merchants were, and this was where the money was.

People pulled back into doorways as he walked by. He didn't notice them, didn't care.

A hotel employee was sweeping the front steps of the Dodge House as he went up. The man stepped aside and watched him.

The desk clerk was sorting out mail behind

the counter. The Colonel didn't see anyone in the lobby; it was still early for most of the guests to be about. He walked to the desk and prodded the clerk's back with his swagger stick.

"I'm looking for Ned Coster's widow," he said coldly. "I understand she's staying here."

The clerk was still shaken from last night's shootings. He gulped, face pale, and managed to say: 'Yes . . . she's upstairs . . . Marshal Ryatt's room . . ."

"Which?"

The clerk pointed nervously. "Room twenty-five . . ."

He didn't move from behind his desk as the Colonel turned and headed for the broad carpeted stairway.

Sadie was still in bed when the Colonel opened the door and stepped inside. She was staring up at the ceiling, her eyes bright. She was floating on a pink cloud, far above everything, feeling no pain.

The Colonel stopped by the bed.

"Get dressed," he said. It was an order.

She turned her head to him and stared. It took a while for her to come back. Slowly the Colonel's thin, stern features came into focus . . . his eyes flinty, brooking no disobedience.

She gasped; cowering under the covers. Terror churned inside her.

He prodded her with the point of his

swagger stick. "Let's go!"

She pulled the cover down from her face. "Go . . . where?"

His smile was wintry. "The Lady Gay. Where you belong!"

The terror mounted. "I . . . I can't . . ." She was frightened of this man. Few men frightened Sadie. This one did. He looked at her not as a woman. He looked at her as if she was a thing . . . something used, of no account.

He reached down to pull back the covers. She grabbed his wrist. "Please . . . no . . ." She shivered at the look in his eyes. "I . . . I'm not dressed . . ."

He wasn't surprised. He shrugged, turned his back to her, and walked to the door.

"Hurry!"

Sadie slipped out of bed and ran to the closet. She got into a dress, stockings, and shoes. Her legs were rubbery, her mouth dry.

"Luke," she whispered. *"Oh, my God, Luke . . ."*

The Colonel opened the door and pointed at her with his swagger stick. She didn't dare disobey. She knew no one would lift a hand to help her.

She went out of the room, ahead of him.

17

A few miles out of the Johnson-Resko camp Ryatt hit a wagon road heading in the direction he was going. He pulled up and looked back. He thought he heard shots, but he wasn't sure. He couldn't see anything.

He followed the wagon road to Little Coon Creek. The Corby place lay just beyond, part of it bottom land, fenced and ploughed, its cornstalks withering in the sun.

The wagon road followed the creek into the farmyard. Ryatt looked around. The ranchhouse was on his left, small and sod-roofed. It was not as big as the barn farther down, which was flanked by a cedar-pole corral. The corral was empty.

A woman had lived in the house. There were curtains in the windows, flower beds under them. A child's swing hanging from the branches of a tree.

Behind the barn a windmill pumped water through a rusting pipe and into a dug-out watering hole for stock. Most of the time Little Coon Creek ran dry. The blades turned slowly in the morning breeze, creaking, the housing needing grease.

Ryatt saw no signs of life. The cows, hogs, and chickens that had belonged to the Corbys had either been sold off or run off after Jeff's death.

Fred Gelson was right, Luke thought; there was nothing here worth anything. The farm was too isolated and in constant danger of Indian attack. Someday, maybe, this land would be worth money. But not now. . . .

Still, Morry had wanted this place . . . wanted it badly enough to buy it from Jeff's widow. Why? He couldn't use it.

He glanced up as he rode toward the barn. A rope still dangled from the beam jutting out of the loft opening. The same rope from which Ned Coster had been found hanging?

Ryatt dismounted, led his horse inside the barn. He wanted to look around the place —

He heard an animal snort inside. He whirled, his hand flashing down to his holster, coming up with it, levelled, the hammer under his right thumb.

It took a few seconds for his eyes to adjust to the gloom inside. He saw the horse, a big bay, saddled and hitched to a support post. Ryatt's gaze searched the barn, but he saw nothing else. There was a ladder leading to the loft. He went up it, slowly, gun ready.

The loft was empty.

He came down and walked to the bay. The animal turned his head to watch as Ryatt approached, then snorted nervously. Ryatt said: "Easy, feller . . ." and ran the palm of his hand down the bay's flank.

Still warm.

Someone had gotten here just ahead of him, someone who must have spotted him riding along the wagon road. The man was somewhere, waiting. Ryatt looked up the loft again. He could hear nothing. In the stillness a man's breathing made sound. Whoever had come here ahead of him was not in the barn.

He tied his roan inside a stall, away from the bay. The big animal was nervous, and the roan had a mean streak. Luke didn't want them tangling.

The barndoors sagged on rusted hinges. One of them had been pushed open just enough to let a rider through. Ryatt left it that way as he went out.

He was ten feet from the barn when he sensed someone watching him from inside the house. He could feel it and knew there was nothing he could do about it now.

Unless . . .

He crossed the yard to the well, his back to the house. He walked slowly, like a man searching for something. The skin between Ryatt's shoulders prickled . . . cold sweat beaded his upper lip.

The well had a wooden enclosure, a safety precaution for small children. The windlass-powered oak bucket hung motionless in the noon stillness just above the well opening.

For a moment Ryatt tried picturing Jeff Corby living here. Farming. A man with a wife and two kids. Not Jeff Corby . . . small, wiry, an expert with explosives. Unsocial — not much of a hand with women.

And then there had been Ned Coster — raunchy, restless, and hard drinking. Two men as different from one another as night from day. What had they in common here . . . ?

The tingling down his spine brought Ryatt back to awareness of his predicament. He knew who was inside that house, a rifle trained on his back. He knew he had only one chance to stay alive.

He crouched down by the well housing, forcing himself to act like a man who thought he was alone. He started to pry loose one of the boards of the well housing.

Morry Teague said harshly: "It's not there, Ryatt!" His voice was clipped, hard. "I looked!"

Ryatt straightened, turned slowly. The belly gun pressed hard against his stomach. It would do him no good now.

The big cattle buyer was standing in the farm-house doorway, his rifle covering Ryatt. He looked angry, frustrated, his expensive "JB" hat pushed back on his head, his big shoulders stiff.

Ryatt let his hands hang down by his sides.

"What are we looking for, Morry?"

Morry took a step out into the yard. "You know damn well what I mean," he snarled. "Coster told you, didn't he? That's the real reason you came to Dodge. Taking the marshal's job was just a blind, wasn't it?"

Ryatt waited, not saying anything.

Morry walked toward him, rifle cocked. "That's why you're out here now. You know where the money is!"

Ryatt shrugged. He was judging the big man's anger, wondering if he could beat the odds.

"I don't know what you're talking about," he said. "What money?"

Morry stopped, a shadow falling across his face. "You mean you —" He swallowed the rest of it, caution holding his tongue. A scowl pinched his heavy features. "What are you doing out here then?"

Ryatt shrugged. "Wanted to look around." His voice was casual. "Ran into a couple of your boys a ways back. Johnson and Resko. They're looking for you."

Morry considered this. Maybe he had talked too much. Maybe the marshal didn't know about the money.

He made a motion with his rifle. "Case you haven't heard, I bought this place from Jeff's widow. That's why I'm here. I want you off it — now!"

Ryatt said: "Sure. No sense in staying —"

The two riders came around the far end of the corral. They pulled up abruptly as they spotted Morry and Ryatt in the yard, Barney jerking at his rifle scabbard, trying to get the big Sharps free.

Morry whirled, fired.

Barney tipped over in the saddle, dropping the rifle. Rafe slid out of his saddle, taking his Winchester with him. He ducked behind the outhouse just as Morry fired again.

Ryatt crouched behind the well housing, gun drawn, ready. He didn't want to kill Morry unless he was forced to.

The big man had turned and was running toward the barn. Rafe's rifle cracked. Morry stumbled and went down, rifle flying. He started to crawl toward the barn opening now only a few yards away.

Ryatt straightened and fired at Rafe, driving him back to cover. He cursed his carelessness in not making sure about the two men he had seen earlier. Rafe and Barney must have followed him from Dodge.

He emptied one of his Colts at Rafe, his bullets splintering boards. He knew he couldn't stay here. Rafe had the advantage with his Winchester.

Morry was hit bad. But he was still crawling toward the safety of the barn.

Ryatt jammed his empty Colt in his holster, drew his left hand gun, and broke away from the well housing, firing a shot at the outhouse as he ran to Morry. He paused just long enough to hook his fingers into the big man's coat collar. He dragged him into the barn just as a bullet kicked up dirt inches from Morry's dragging heels.

Ryatt eased Morry down and looked around. The barn would provide only temporary safety — it was also a trap. Outside, it was quiet. Barney had been hit. Rafe was probably thinking things over. Ryatt figured he would have a few moments to consider his own course of action.

He pulled the wounded cattle buyer up to a stall that once had housed Jeff's milk cow and sat Morry up, his back against the side board. Farther on Ryatt's rented roan jerked at his reins, whistling nervously.

Ryatt crouched beside Morry and pulled the big man's coat away from the bullet hole in his side. It looked bad. Not much he could do for the man.

Morry's eyes flickered and stared into Ryatt's face. His lips twisted with pain, with bitter anger.

"Friends of yours, Ryatt?"

Ryatt's voice was cold. "Hardly."

He turned toward the door as Rafe's voice, carried. "Hey, Marshal! Got a proposition for you. Want to hear it?"

Ryatt didn't answer. Morry's breathing was shallow. He ran his tongue over his lips and coughed. A bright trickle of blood came down the side of his mouth.

"No sense in killing each other over it," Rafe continued. "What do you say? Three-way split?"

Ryatt looked down at Morry. "What's he talking about, Morry?"

"Money . . ." The big man had trouble talking. "Money Jeff and Ned Coster stole from me. Money they got buried somewhere around here . . ."

"How much?"

"Enough." Morry coughed again, blood showing on his lips.

"And you thought I knew where it was?"

Morry nodded. "Why else would Coster have —"

A shot ripped through the barn door and caromed off the blade of a ploughshare, whining as it smashed its way out through the back of the barn. The horses reared, shrilling with fright. The bay broke loose and began to run toward the door. Ryatt headed him off and grabbed the trailing reins. He was dragged almost into the opening before he pulled the bay around and walked him back to the support post. He made sure he was well tied this time.

"Got you cornered!" Rafe yelled. "No way you can get out of this, Ryatt. Goddammit, make up your mind!"

Morry began to laugh . . . a hurt, bitter laugh. "You don't know where it is, do you?"

Ryatt nodded. "I never did."

"Gave them both a job helping out at the feed lots," Morry said. "Jeff wasn't doing too well here, and his wife was getting restless. He needed money . . . figured he'd lose her . . . guess he would have, anyway. Amy's not the kind who . . . who . . ." He coughed again, this time a convulsive spell that left him spent, eyes glazed.

"Jeff and Coster robbed you?" There was surprise in Ryatt's voice.

Morry nodded. "Blew the safe one night . . . burglar-proof, they told me . . . hardest steel in . . ." He sucked in a deep, ragged breath. "Blew the door clean off its hinges . . ."

"But you kept it quiet," Ryatt said. "Why?"

"Had to. Money I was holding out on the company. I couldn't let them know . . ."

"Who killed Ned Coster?"

Morry's head rolled. "Not me. Would have been a fool to. Jeff was dead. Only Ned knew —"

Rafe's harsh voice cut in: "We're not playing games out here, Marshal! You got five minutes to think it over. Then we'll burn you out!"

Ryatt went to the door, keeping out of sight. "We?"

"Barney and me!"

Ryatt sneered. "Barney's dead."

Rafe laughed. "Show him, Barney!"

There was a moment's stillness, then Barney's big Sharps boomed, the heavy slug smashing into the door, narrowly missing Morry as it ripped into the stall boards.

Barney's voice lifted; it sounded hurt, but determined. "Want another sample, Marshal?"

Ryatt considered his alternatives. He had little choice.

"All right," he called out. "Three-way split!"

Behind him Morry said: "You sonuvabitch! You told me you didn't know . . ."

He was dying. He made one last effort, trying to get to his shoulder gun. He got it out just as Ryatt turned back to him. Ryatt smashed a fist into the man's face. Morry's head banged against the stall boards. He slumped down on his side.

"Sorry," Ryatt muttered. He picked up Morry's gun and slipped it inside his waistband, next to the derringer.

He walked to the door and said: "I'm coming out."

"What about Morry?"

"He's dead."

There was a moment's silence, then: "Throw your guns outside. Morry's too. He wears one in a shoulder holster." Rafe's voice was flat, deadly. "Don't try any tricks, Marshal. I know them all. Just come out with both hands clasped on your head!"

Ryatt unbuckled his cartridge belts and

tossed them out into the yard. He took Morry's .38 and threw it out, too. He waited a moment before walking out, his hands clasped over his flat-crowned hat.

Rafe came away from the outhouse, rifle held ready, a wary glint in his eyes. Barney was leaning against the corral bars, the big Sharps butt down at his feet.

Rafe glanced past Ryatt toward the barn. "You sure he's dead?"

"Why don't you go see?"

Rafe's eyes glittered angrily. "Drag him out here!" he said. "I'll be right behind you."

Ryatt shrugged. He walked back into the barn, bent over Morry's inert figure and dragged the big man out into the yard.

Rafe looked down at the cattle buyer and spat. Morry groaned slightly. Rafe tilted his rifle muzzle at the man's head.

Ryatt said grimly: "Let him be!"

Rafe looked at him, eyes ugly. "He ain't dead."

"Just about." Ryatt made a gesture, his eyes flinty. "You want the money?"

Rafe shrugged. "Yeah — guess we're wasting time." He turned away from Morry. "Where is it?"

Ryatt walked across the yard to the well housing, Rafe following. He looked at Ryatt and scowled.

"Here?"

Ryatt nodded.

Rafe's mouth twisted. "Shee-yit! We looked all through that well housing!" He swung his rifle muzzle around to level at Ryatt's chest. "If you're stalling — ?"

"You didn't look in the right place," Ryatt cut in. "Coster sent me a wire, told me just where he hid it."

"One-armed bastid!" Rafe muttered. "He told you . . . wouldn't tell us —"

"So you killed him?"

"Not me. The Colonel." Rafe grinned. "Put a rope around his neck and asked him for the last time where they hid the money. Ned was as ornery as a jug-headed mule. Claimed he didn't know where the money was. The Colonel lost patience, pushed him out . . ."

He looked past Ryatt as Barney yelled: "What are you gabbing about, Rafe?" He was coming toward them, holding his side. He leaned against the side of the barn for a moment. Ryatt figured the kid was hurt more than he was letting on.

"Come on, Rafe," Barney called. "Get the money and let's all get the hell out of here. Before the Colonel comes looking for us."

Rafe nodded. "All right," he growled to Ryatt. "You say it's hidden in there — you find it!"

He took a couple of steps back from the marshal, cocked his rifle. "One thing, Ryatt — you come up empty and you're dead!"

Ryatt crouched down by the well housing. Behind Rafe Morry stirred . . . one last flicker of life in him. He opened his eyes and saw his rifle lying a few feet from him. He rolled over, reaching for it . . .

Barney was watching Rafe and Ryatt. He saw Morry move out of the corners of his eyes and yelled wildly: "Rafe . . . look out . . . behind you . . . —"

He brought the Sharps up, wincing as he did. His attention was on Morry, and his shot smashed into the cattle buyer.

Ryatt killed Rafe as the burly man stood, half turned away from him, distracted by Barney's yell. He shot the Texan twice with his derringer then grabbed Rafe's rifle as the man staggered and started to fall. It was already cocked. He blew Barney's head off with it.

Morry was still alive when Ryatt bent over him. Maybe he'd live long enough for Ryatt to get him back to Dodge . . .

18

Gauzy afternoon clouds thinned the sun's rays. The people of Dodge watched Luke Ryatt ride into town, leading three horses, each of them burdened by a body slung across a saddle. One was still alive — the other two were dead.

The marshal pulled up in front of the Polke Funeral House. Smaller lettering announced that the Polkes also did custom carpentry — cabinets and furniture made to order.

A small crowd gathered around Ryatt. Angus came hurrying up with Mayor Kelly — both men had been in the barbershop when Luke rode by. Farther down, Fred Gelson was crossing the street to join them.

Kelly went up to one of the bodies dangling across the bay's saddle and whirled saying: "Morry!" He looked up at Ryatt, shocked and angered. "My God, Ryatt — this is going too far! This is beyond all —"

Ryatt cut him off. "I didn't kill him! Get him to a doctor. Fast! Morry'll tell you who shot him, if he lives that long!"

The Polke Funeral House was a family

business. Young Rabel Polke, as thin and cadaverous-looking as his father, came out and took charge of the bodies.

Kelly said angrily: "I'll talk to you later, Ryatt!" He and Fred Gelson went into the funeral parlor with Morry while someone ran to fetch Doctor Hayden.

Angus remained behind with Ryatt.

"I don't know what happened," he said slowly. "But I think this calls for a drink." He smiled and shrugged. "Some explanations too, Marshal."

Ryatt nodded. He owed Angus that much.

They went into the Long Branch Saloon, stood up at the bar. The place was not crowded. The bartender came up to serve them.

"Same as always, Ernie," Angus said. He looked at Ryatt. "Scotch?"

Ryatt nodded. It was no time to be particular.

"There's going to be a lot of hell raised," Angus said. "Morry was a big man around here. It'll probably go all the way up to the Governor's office."

"I didn't shoot him."

Angus studied the tall, hard-faced marshal, nodding slowly. "I believe you. Where did it happen?"

"Jeff Corby's place."

"The Corby farm?" Angus ran his fingers through his side whiskers. "What was Morry doing out there?"

156

"Same as I was," Ryatt said. His tone was casual, short. "Looking for money Jeff had buried out there."

Angus shook his head. "You're kidding! Hell, everybody in town knew Jeff was poor as a churchmouse —"

"Not his money," Ryatt said. He finished his drink and set the empty glass down on the bar.

Angus wasn't satisfied. "Whose then?"

"Morry's."

Angus didn't understand. "You're crazy! Why would Morry hide money on Jeff's place —"

"Ask him," Ryatt said. "Ask him why he bought Jeff's farm from the Corby widow this morning."

He glanced at the wall clock. He didn't have much time left. Be dark soon enough, and the Colonel was waiting for him.

"How's the town?"

"Quiet," Angus muttered. "Everyone's waiting to see what you're going to do."

Ryatt looked at him, face hard.

"Face up to the Colonel," Angus muttered, "or run . . ."

Ryatt's smile was frosty. "I'm going to earn my fee, Angus."

Angus sighed. He called for another drink, but Ryatt said to count him out. "One's my limit for today."

He left Angus at the bar and stepped outside.

It was a pleasant late afternoon. The breeze blowing in from the river was mild. The air was bright, clean . . . the sun lowering on the horizon.

A good time, Ryatt decided, to see Amy Corby.

Ryatt knocked on the door and waited for what seemed to be a long time before Amy's sister came to answer the door. Rena was not happy to see him. She said quite coldly that Amy was not in.

Ryatt said he didn't believe her. He kept his tone pleasant, but firm. Maybe he should come inside and see for himself.

This alarmed the angular woman. "Amy's at the railroad station, checking her baggage," she said. "She's leaving for St. Louis on the morning train."

It was a five minute walk to the Santa Fe station. Ryatt ran into Amy as she was coming out. Her brother-in-law Will was with her. He still looked like a slob in overalls.

"I hear you're leaving, Mrs. Corby," Ryatt said.

She nodded, her eyes hiding an uneasiness. "Yes, tomorrow."

He looked at Will standing to one side, his hands in his pockets. The man looked uncomfortable.

Ryatt grinned. "Alone, Mrs. Corby?"

She frowned. "Of course."

Ryatt shrugged. "I thought you might be having company."

Anger reddened her cheeks. "You're insulting, Marshal!" She started to walk past him, head held high.

He looked after her. "I found out why Jeff went to the Lady Gay that night."

She stopped and then turned slowly around to face him. "I don't care," she said. "Not any more."

"You should," Ryatt said evenly. "It concerns a lot of money."

She stiffened, her upper lip twitching. Then she gained control of herself. "Money?" Her smile was sweetly tender. "You must be mistaken, Marshal. Jeff never had more than five dollars in hard cash in his pocket at any given time."

"He did three weeks ago," Ryatt said. He touched fingers to the brim of his hat. "Good day, Mrs. Corby."

He turned away.

"Marshal!"

He looked at her. "I'll tell you all about it tomorrow," he said. "It might interest you, before you leave."

There was no one in the room when Ryatt checked in at the Dodge House. He washed, changed clothes, checked his guns, and made sure his string tie was straight. Downstairs he asked the desk clerk about Sadie.

"She went out," the clerk answered. He looked nervous, ill at ease. "The man they call the Colonel . . . he came to get her."

Ryatt took this calmly enough.

He went into the dining room. It was early for supper, but the cook fixed him something. Ryatt ate by himself and had a cigar with his coffee.

The sun went down. The shadows crept across the river, enfolding the town. One of the waiters began lighting the ceiling chandeliers.

Kelly came in with Lorry Gray, Fred Gelson and Angus MacIntosh. Kelly was grim-faced as they walked up to Ryatt's table.

"Morry's dead!" Kelly announced. His tone was harsh, accusing. "He never recovered consciousness."

"Sorry to hear it," Ryatt answered.

"You killed him?"

Ryatt looked up at the angry Mayor, and frowned. "Why should I have?"

"Because Morry was pushing you to do something about the Colonel!" Kelly snapped.

Ryatt leaned back in his chair. "If that's what you want to believe — ?"

"Goddammit!" Kelly snapped. "Morry's dead. I'm going to have a hell of a lot of explaining to do to a lot of important people. Why I ever let Ned Coster talk me into hiring you in the first place —"

"Yeah," Ryatt cut in, his voice a slow, dangerous drawl. "Why did you, Kelly?"

Angus said quickly: "For Chrissakes, Luke, don't make it hard for us!"

Ryatt's eyes narrowed. "Make it hard for what?" His cold gaze traveled over each man, holding.

"We made a mistake," Kelly answered. His ruddy face had a deeper coloring than usual, his blue eyes almost electric in their intensity. "The mistake was in hiring!"

Lorry Gray nodded assent, his pale, watery gray eyes uneasy. "I never voted for you," he muttered.

Gelson shrugged. "Not my idea, either."

Angus remained silent.

"Looks like we're all agreed," Kelly said grimly. He extended his hand to Ryatt. "I'll take that badge back now, Luke."

Ryatt's voice was flinty. "What about the Colonel and those Texans holed up in the Lady Gay?"

"Morry's dead. No way the Colonel's going to get any more money from him now. They'll probably leave."

"No!" Ryatt's voice was flat, uncompromising.

"It was our mistake," Kelly muttered. "We'll pay you what we agreed. Just hand over that badge and get out of town."

"I'm not finished here," Ryatt said bleakly.

"Far as we're concerned, you are!"

Ryatt got to his feet. Kelly backed off a bit at the look in Ryatt's eyes.

"I took on a job," Ryatt said coldly. "I never leave without finishing!"

19

Sadie sprawled in a chair inside the Lady Gay, her hair straggling down over her eyes. Whiskey dribbled down a corner of her slack mouth. She raised a hand, bruise marks showing above her elbow, and slowly wiped the trickle away.

"Please . . ." she whispered. She was hurt, frightened . . . the terror inside her growing. "Please . . . no more . . ."

The Colonel eyed her disapprovingly. He was sitting across from her, at a table against the back wall. He looked at her the way someone would regard a fly annoying him with its buzzing, or a cockroach skittering across the floor.

She was nothing to him. Her body didn't interest him. He didn't consider her as a woman. Her dress had been ripped away. Sadie clung to what was left, holding some of the fabric against her. A firm, white breast showed, nipple dark red, swollen. He didn't even see it.

The others watched from a distance. Five trail-hardened Texans who had come to

Dodge with the Colonel. They didn't share the Colonel's straight-laced views of women; they didn't like what he was doing. They didn't dare interfere.

The Colonel picked up the bottle of whiskey, refilled Sadie's glass, and pushed it across the table to her.

Sadie shrank away from it. Her gaze was blur-ring, her voice slurring: "No . . . no more . . ."

"Drink it!" It was a cold, implacable order.

She rolled her head, and tried to stand up. Her legs were rubbery. They crumpled under her, and she slid back, falling face down across the table, one hand knocking the glass to the floor.

The Colonel stood up and eyed her for a moment, his anger cold and burning. He grabbed her by the hair and jerked her head up. Pain opened Sadie's mouth. He picked up the bottle and poured whiskey into it.

Sadie choked, gasped. She moaned, a small, pitiful cry . . . a frightened whimper.

He shoved her back into her chair.

"Where is it?"

Her eyes blurred and unfocused, searched for him. She had more than half a bottle of raw whiskey in her. Women talked when they were drunk. Like men, they babbled of things they wouldn't reveal when sober.

"Where did Jeff and Coster hide the money?"

Her head rolled weakly. "I . . . I don't know . . ."

He grabbed her by the hair again, jerking her toward him. She knew, damn it! She had to know!

"Where?"

But Sadie was past all hearing now, past caring. He shook her roughly, then let her go. She slumped forward across the table.

He stood over her, frustrated. Outside a Santa Fe switch engine clanged as it went by, steam venting, billowing up against the dying day.

One of the men watching from a corner table said: "Well, Colonel — maybe she doesn't know."

The Colonel shrugged. He straightened his tunic, walked across the room to the front door, and looked outside. The red glow of sunset was paling to aquamarine in the west . . . the shadows beginning to pool in the street. In the south a star appeared, bright and solitary.

That was the way home, he thought — that way lay Texas. A bitterness burned in him, rising like bile in his throat. He didn't belong here in this Yankee town, a thousand miles from home.

Rory Starbuck, a red-bearded giant, joined

him. He knew what the Colonel was thinking and shared it.

"Not much to go back home for," he muttered.

The Colonel was silent, staring out into the darkening street, staring into a bleak and bitter future.

"That sonuvabitching marshal got Barney and Rafe," Starbuck went on, his voice hardening. "You figger he'll be coming here next?"

The Colonel nodded. "He'll come."

Starbuck shifted and slid his hand down over his holstered gun. He had a small ranch back in Texas that he ran alone; he had no other ties. Only the Colonel . . .

"Guess he will," Starbuck said. "But I'm not waiting, Colonel."

The Colonel turned slowly and eyed him, disappointment showing.

"You running?"

"Hell, you know me better than that." Starbuck spat out into the street. "We been talking . . . me, Lee, and Riber. We don't like sitting here, waiting. We figgered we'd go out after Ryatt first."

"That's what Rafe and Barney did," the Colonel pointed out. "You saw what happened to them."

Starbuck shrugged. "Not that way." He chewed on a wood match, strong white teeth showing in a hard grin. "We're figgering on ambushing the bastid."

The Colonel frowned. "Where?"

"I'll be up on the roof," Starbuck replied. "Lee and Riber will slip out the back door; it's just about dark enough now. Lee will wait for him in the alley, watching the street. Riber will be down by the railroad station . . ."

The Colonel nodded, his smile cold. "Crossfire."

"Wiped out half a company of Union jacks that way," Starbuck said. "Just three of us, cut off from our platoon . . . up on Sawyer's Ridge . . ."

The big redhead was silent then, the memory of that battle won coming back. A bittersweet victory, lost in the aftermath of defeat. Hurt glowed briefly in his eyes, then faded. He turned to go.

"It's chancy," the Colonel said. "I know Ryatt. He's no fool."

Starbuck shrugged. "Better than sitting here, waiting . . ."

He went back to the table where Lee Spinner and Riber were waiting.

"Rory!"

Starbuck paused, then turned to look back to the Colonel. The tall man's face showed no emotion; his eyes were cold. But his voice carried what neither showed.

"Happy hunting, Rory!"

He stood by the open door and watched

them go — Starbuck up the stairs to the roof; Lee Spinner, cold, taciturn, and Riber, one-time sharecropper, twice decorated by the Confederacy, out the back door.

The light faded out of the western sky; the shadows were heavy now in the street. The Colonel stirred and walked back to the table where Sadie lay slumped, snoring in a drunken stupor. He stood over her for a moment, thinking things over — then he reached down and prodded her bare shoulder urgently.

She stirred and looked up, her eyes bleary.

"You slept with him," he pursued grimly. "Men talk. Coster must have told you something."

She sighed and closed her eyes. "I told you . . . Ned said nothing to me. I never even knew about the money . . . not until Morry —"

"*Morry!*"

Sadie nodded, her mouth slack. She ran her tongue across her dry lips. "Morry thought Ryatt knew . . ." She hesitated, sucking in a deep breath, regrouping her hazy thoughts. "He thought Ned had told Ryatt where he and Jeff had hidden the money. I don't even know what money he meant. Morry never told me that. But he promised me a hundred dollars if I found out where they had hidden it, a ticket to Denver . . ."

The Colonel's voice was a whiplash, cold

and threatening. "Well?"

"He doesn't know . . ." Sadie's head rolled; it was an effort for her to think, to talk. "If he does . . . Ryatt, I mean . . . he keeps it to himself. He . . . he never told me . . ."

"You're lying!"

She shrank away from him. "I swear . . . I don't know . . . I'd tell you if I did . . ."

The Colonel considered this. It could be she was telling the truth. But Jeff Corby and Ned Coster were dead. Only they had known where they had hidden the money.

He ran the only other possibility through his mind. There was still the chance Ryatt knew. It was even possible he already had the money. Something had happened out there at Jeff's place. Barney and Rafe had been sent out to find out. They couldn't talk now. And Morry Teague was dead. The Colonel faced that bitter fact; there was no way now they could force the cattle buyer into coming up with the money he still owed them.

He couldn't go back to Texas empty-handed. He couldn't start over again; he didn't want to. He needed that money Jeff and Coster had stolen from Morry. He wasn't leaving Dodge without it.

He prodded Sadie roughly, his voice harsh. "Stand up!"

Sadie lifted her head, shivering at the threat in his voice. "Please . . . I told you . . ."

He grabbed her by the hair and jerked her erect. She cried out in pain, the remnants of clothing dropping away from her. She stood by the table, moaning, terrified. "Oh, my god, no . . ."

The Colonel finished tearing the dress from her. She made no effort to cover herself.

The Colonel stepped back and turned to the two men left in the Lady Gay. Jerdney Smith was behind the bar — tall, lanky, an unsmiling man. He and Ed Brawley were half brothers; they generally stuck together.

"Get a hammer, nails and some rope," the Colonel ordered. "I want her tied up!" He levelled his swagger stock. "Over there, against that wall, facing the door!"

He watched as Jerdney drove heavy nails into the wall and tied up the numbed, naked woman, her hands outstretched, like a crucifixion.

There was little doubt in the Colonel's mind that Ryatt would be coming. Ryatt had an odd sense of honor concerning women he had slept with.

It was possible that the marshal would get by Starbuck, Lee, and Riber. The Colonel's eyes were cold. He would need an edge when Luke Ryatt came in after him.

That's why he wanted Sadie there — that's who he wanted Ryatt to see first when he came busting into the Lady Gay!

20

Lorry Gray came walking up to the counter at his clerk's request, trying to look stern, angry — trying to show an authority he did not possess. From behind the store counter, the clerk stared uneasily at the tall man with the marshal's badge pinned to his black coat.

There was no one else inside the store. The last customer had gone home.

"We're closing up," Lorry said. His tone was uncivil and curt. He had sided with the Mayor. He didn't like the turn things had taken, and he was worried about what Morry Teague's killing would bring.

"Go ahead, close up," Ryatt said. His voice was even. "Just give me what I ordered, then I'll leave."

Lorry Gray glanced at his clerk.

"Six sticks of dynamite," the clerk muttered. His voice was strained.

"Caps and fuses," Ryatt added coldly.

Gray's watery eyes blinked. "Sorry," he said harshly. "We don't carry dynamite."

It was a lie. Most general merchandise stores stocked dynamite, even in farm country. It was useful for blasting stumps and rock ledges, and for digging wells . . .

Ryatt started toward the back door. "Let's go see," he said grimly.

Gray stiffened. "Just a minute, Ryatt!"

He blocked off the door, facing the town marshal. "I don't have to sell you anything! And you no longer have any authority here. Far as I'm concerned, you're no longer an employee of this city —"

Ryatt's right hand brushed his coat skirt aside, revealing the butt of his holstered Colt.

"Speaking of authority —"

Gray's face paled. "You wouldn't — ?"

Ryatt shrugged. "Why not?" His voice was soft, uncaring. It sent a shiver through the storekeeper and the clerk who was watching.

"Frank," Gray said, his voice clogging with fear, "get the marshal what he ordered."

He backed away from the counter, turned quickly, and made an ungraceful exit through a side door. Ryatt waited until the clerk went into the store room, then turned his back to the counter and slanted a look through the store window. It was dark enough outside to get lamps burning.

He speculated briefly about Sadie. He wondered if she had gone willingly with the Colonel and what her business could have been with him. The Dodge House desk clerk had not said.

Besides, he thought, no one north of the

deadline in Dodge cared much about what happened to women like Sadie.

Frank came back with his six sticks of dynamite, primer caps, and fuses. He handled the stocks gingerly, but Ryatt knew there was little need for that much caution. There was slight danger from those yellow-wrapped sticks if a man knew what he was doing and didn't allow himself to get careless.

"Wrap them up," he instructed.

The clerk tore a length of brown paper from a roll and carefully wrapped the dynamite in it.

He put the order on the counter, hesitated and then made out a sales slip.

Ryatt signed it and said: "Charged to the city . . ." He picked up the small package and went outside.

Front Street was deserted. Shops were closed, windows dark. Ryatt knew people were watching and waiting from behind closed doors.

He carried the package tucked under his left arm. Cartridge belts crossing, holsters thonged down on his thighs. His belly gun pressing hard against the lean flatness of his stomach.

Tools of his trade.

He paused on the edge of the plankwalk in front of Gray's store and looked down the street toward the deadline. Behind him a bolt snicked as Frank locked up; a moment later the store lights went out.

Ryatt had counted seven men in the Lady Gay with the Colonel. He had eliminated two of them — Rafe and Barney. That left five.

Five trail-hardened Texans — tough, armed. Waiting for him, knowing he was coming.

Angus intercepted him as Ryatt started his walk down the street toward the Lady Gay.

"You don't stand a chance," Angus said. "Luke, listen! Take the money. You earned it. Leave town. Now!"

The man was serious. Ryatt appreciated his concern.

"Can't," he said shortly. "Job's not finished."

It was beyond Angus.

"You're a goddam, stubborn fool!" he said. "You've got the town against you. Most of them wouldn't mind seeing you killed —"

Ryatt's look went through him, stopping the Scotsman.

Angus sighed. "Well, for what's it's worth, I believe you. About Morry. You didn't kill him. I'll testify to that."

"Thanks," Ryatt said. His voice was dry, unimpressed. He walked away.

The board sign on the far side of the street faced Ryatt as he walked toward the deadline. No weapons carried, north OR south of the deadline!

Luke's smile was wintry. For what it was

worth, he had made that order stick. For a few days, anyway.

He stepped out into the still muddy street, cutting in front of the sign and crossing the railroad tracks, turning south then, in the direction of the Lady Gay. It was full dark now. Up ahead a lamp hung on a switch handle, amber glass glowing. In the distance, lights showed in the windows of the railroad station.

He kept to the far side of the rails, a shadow moving unnoticed against the night. There was a toolshed up ahead. He had spotted it earlier, the first time he had come to the Lady Gay, and had filed it away in the back of his head. Small kegs of iron railroad spikes flanked the shed. A stack of railroad ties loomed up just beyond.

Ryatt cut back across the rails, stopping by the shed. The Lady Gay was just across the street. The door was closed. A light showed against the dirty windows. He could not see through them.

Ryatt paused, leaned his shoulder against the side of the toolshed, and judged the intervening distance. The street was wide here, the Lady Gay separated from the railroad tracks by fifty, maybe sixty yards. He figured it would be no problem.

A shadow moved in an alley across the street, a rifle momentarily reflecting a glint of starlight. Ryatt was down on one knee, unwrapping the small package. He did not notice.

Another shadow moved slowly along the tracks, coming toward him from the railroad station.

Ryatt picked up two sticks of dynamite, capped them, and short-fused them, tying them in one small bundle. A ten-second fuse. His eye told him. He had done this sort of thing before.

Two sticks should do it; the other four were for emergencies.

He plucked a cigar from his vest pocket, clamped his lips over it, and burned a match on his thumbnail.

Lee Spinner, coming down the tracks, saw the match flare and fired. The bullet hit Ryatt in the side as he stood up, driving him back against the toolshed.

He dropped the dynamite and turned. He saw Spinner running toward him along the tracks, just ahead of a switch engine rolling up from a yard spur onto the main line.

The engineer spotted the running figure in the engine's headlight. He yelled out and jerked on his whistle cord.

Ryatt drew and fired just as Spinner, startled, started to swerve away from the oncoming engine. Lee staggered and fell across the tracks. The engineer hauled back desperately on his brake lever. The train's drive wheels locked and screamed on the iron rails, sparks flying. The front trucks rolled over Lee's limp body and went on for another fifty yards before grinding to a halt.

The engineer reversed the drive wheels, steam venting, billowing across the tracks and the toolshed. The engine backed up, gathering speed. The engineer saw what was left of Lee as he leaned out of his cab window; he threw up.

The man in the alley had started running across the street, toward the toolshed. Ryatt didn't see him. He crouched, picked up the dynamite he had dropped and staggered away from the shed just as Starbuck stood up in plain view on the roof of the Lady Gay and fired down at him. The bullets ripped into the toolshed, glanced off something inside and screamed into the darkness behind the marshal.

Ryatt gritted his teeth, steadying himself. He touched the fuse to his lighted cigar, drew his arm back, pain stabbing through his side, and let it fly . . .

The dynamite arced up against the night. It hit the parapet to one side of Starbuck and skidded over onto the flat roof behind him. It caught Starbuck by surprise. He hesitated a moment too long before turning and making a dive for the dynamite bundle.

The blast lighted the sky above the Lady Gay!

Riber, halfway across the street, skidded to

a stop, turning a shocked look upward.

Ryatt pumped three shots into him.

Rifles opened up from inside the Lady Gay as Riber sprawled face down in the muddy street. They couldn't see Ryatt. They were firing wildly, bullets screaming off the rails around the marshal, thunking into the stack of ties.

Ryatt dropped to his hands and knees and started crawling away from the toolshed. He left the other four sticks of dynamite behind. He couldn't waste time looking for them. He headed for the railroad station, holding his hand to his side, feeling blood warm and sticky pumping through his fingers. He was lucky this time . . .

He glanced back to the Lady Gay. A small glow was flickering above the shattered roof line. Ryatt didn't know how much damage two sticks of dynamite had caused. But it had taken care of the rifleman on the roof. And now the firing from inside the Lady Gay had stopped, too.

He ran a mental count through his head. Three left. He made it to the station, staggered up the steps, and went inside, pushing past a startled ticket agent.

He looked around the station — closed ticket windows, hardwood benches, and spittoons. A baggageman looked at him from a platform door.

Ryatt sank down on one of the benches and motioned to the ticket agent.

"Get Doc Hayden over here! Make it fast!"

The man spotted the blood, but he reacted faster to the gun in Ryatt's fist. He nodded and ran off.

Ryatt reloaded his Colts. He could feel the pain stabbing like a red hot iron in his side and the blood seeping from the bullet hole.

He made a wad of his handkerchief, pulled his coat off, yanked his bloodied shirttails free of his trousers, and pressed the handkerchief against the wound. He sat bent over, a loaded gun by his side. He watched the door.

The station agent came back with the doctor within five minutes. It seemed longer. Ryatt heard them come up the steps, one of them wheezing from the exertion. He picked up his gun . . .

It should be the doctor, but you could never tell.

The station agent saw the gun in Ryatt's hand. He spun aside, eyes frightened. Doctor Hayden, a short, pudgy man, out of breath, didn't even break stride.

He came up to Ryatt and said brusquely: "Put that goddam gun away!"

Ryatt slid the gun back into its holster.

"Lie down on the bench!"

Ryatt obeyed. Doc Hayden was short on niceties, but he was competent. He had patched up bullet holes before.

"Pretty bad," he said. He looked down into Ryatt's face. "Take a deep breath."

Ryatt did. The pain in his side was steady, burning. But his head was clear.

"Lost a lot of blood," Hayden muttered. "Turn over on your side . . ."

"Just patch it up," Ryatt said grimly. "I'll worry about the blood later."

Doc Hayden ignored him. "Lucky," he said bluntly. "Looks like a clean bullet hole — in and out." He straightened and checked inside his bag. "Isn't the first time you've stopped a bullet, either."

"Won't be the last," Ryatt grated.

The doctor took out a thick bandage roll, a cotton swab, and a jar of carbolic salve. He daubed the swab into the jar and cleaned out the bullet hole. It burned worse than the bullet had. Ryatt gritted his teeth.

Hayden made a thick pad, held it against the two bullet holes, and wound bandages around Ryatt's middle. He finished, stood up, and closed his bag.

"Not much more I can do," he said. "The rest is up to you. A week or two in bed —"

Ryatt cut him off. "Later."

He stood up and picked up his coat. Hayden helped him into it. The bandages felt bulky under his bloody shirt. He buckled his cartridge belts around his waist. They seemed to hang heavier than usual.

"Thanks, doc."

He had a job to finish. He'd worry about bedrest another time.

21

Sadie hung limply against the wall, a thin line of spittle sliding down the corner of her mouth. Her long hair hung down over her breasts. The rope cut cruelly into her wrists. Her knees sagged.

Part of the ceiling had come down in the blast. Plaster made a white film over tables and across the board floor.

The Colonel was standing in the doorway, looking out into the darkness. Riber's body lay motionless in the street. But the Colonel's attention was focussed on the railroad station. He had just seen Doctor Hayden and the railroad ticket agent hurry inside.

There was the smell of wood smoke in the night, the sound of flames crackling. The Colonel didn't stir.

Behind him Jerdney Smith and Ed Brawley came running down the stairs. They crossed to him, faces smoke-blackened, eyes red-rimmed, bleak, bitter.

"Blew a hole through the roof," Jerdney said. "Whole upper floor is a mess. And the fire's spreading . . ." He looked at his half brother. "Nothing we could do about it . . ."

The Colonel didn't look at him. His voice was only mildly curious.

"Starbuck?"

"Not much left of him," Brawley answered. He was a broad, powerful man, his weathered features and steerhorn mustache making him look older than his twenty-seven years. A chaw of tobacco bulged in his right cheek.

"Rory must have been right there when it went off!"

Jerdney Smith swore. "The bastid got them all, Colonel! Barney, Rafe, Lee, Riber, and Starbuck!"

The Colonel turned now and faced the two remaining Texans who had come with him to Dodge . . . men who had shared his hopes and carried their share of the load.

"There's still three of us," he said dryly.

Jerdney shook his head. The crackling from upstairs was growing. Smoke was drifting down the stairs.

"Morry Teague's dead," he muttered. "No way we can get our money now."

It was a statement of fact. No rancor. Just a vocal acceptance of the reality.

The Colonel understood. He shrugged. "Yeah — no sense in staying here." He pointed. "The back way's still clear . . ."

Brawley shifted his weight. "Hell, I'm staying!" His look shamed his half brother. "We came up the trail together. We're going back the same way, or not at all . . ."

Jerdney shrugged. "Girl back home . . . yaller hair, big blue eyes. Said she'd wait . . ."

He shrugged. "Like Ed said, Colonel . . . we go back together, or . . ."

The Colonel nodded. That was all the appreciation he showed, but they understood.

"There's still that money on Jeff's farm," Brawley muttered. "If we could —"

Jerdney was looking out into the night. "Not much chance of that," he said. "Could spend a month digging up the place and never find it."

Brawley sighed. "Reckon there's not much left to go back to, Colonel. Niggers running free, sassing white folks. Carpetbaggers all over the state, telling us what to do . . ."

The smoke was beginning to thicken inside the Lady Gay. The red glare on the roof was lighting the night sky, shadows flickering across the tracks.

Brawley said: "How much did Jeff and Coster take from Morry?"

"Ninety thousand dollars." The Colonel's tone was distant; he was thinking of something else at the moment.

He saw Doctor Hayden come out of the station, bag in hand, and watched him walk back along the rails, heading uptown.

Jerdney's hand came up, a gun in it. The Colonel pushed it aside. "We've got no quarrel with him," he said.

"That sonuvabitching marshal!" Brawley exploded. "Where is he?"

"Inside the railroad station," the Colonel answered. He thought about the money now — how much it meant, split three ways.

He shrugged. "Looks like Riber or Lee got to him. He's hurt, or Doc Hayden wouldn't have gone to him . . ."

Jerdney stared across the night to the station. "Hope he's dying," he said. He turned to the Colonel. "Maybe he won't come —"

"He'll come."

Brawley scowled. "He rode out to Jeff's place, didn't he? Think he knew where the money was?"

"Maybe."

"It's our money," Jerdney said. "We sweated blood for it."

Brawley spat a stream of tobacco juice out into the street. People were gathering north of the deadline, watching the fire. There was no wind. For the moment the flames were confined to the Lady Gay. They did not venture further.

"Beats me," Brawley snarled. "If that goddam marshal found the money, why did he come back?"

The Colonel had been thinking about this.

"Because it's his job," he said. "And because Coster and Jeff were his friends."

Brawley and Jerdney Smith understood this.

"That kind of man, eh?" Jerdney muttered.

The Colonel nodded. "That kind."

He walked slowly back across the room, stopped by Sadie, and ran his cold gaze over her limp figure.

"Cheap little whore," he said.

She raised her head and looked up at him through glassy eyes. Smoke got into her lungs . . . she coughed, the spasm rocking her body.

At the door Brawley suddenly turned, calling: "He's coming, Colonel!"

The Colonel smiled bitterly. "Knew he would."

He motioned the two men to him. "Jerdney — take the end of the bar. Ed — over there."

Jerdney shot a questioning glance to Sadie. "What about her?"

"She's our ace in the hole," the Colonel said.

Brawley sneered: "That floozy . . ."

"Is a woman," the Colonel cut in coldly. "And Ryatt was living with her . . ."

22

Ryatt saw her against the back wall, yellow smoke spreading like a shroud around her limp-hanging figure. Just a cheap little whore who had started out wrong and would end up nowhere . . .

He spotted her as he paused just outside the Lady Gay's open door, and he felt a moment's sharp regret and then a deepening anger. No one should be treated like that, he thought . . . not even a dog.

"I'm coming in, Colonel," he said.

The Colonel's voice answered him. "Come right in, Luke! We're waiting!"

Luke Ryatt stepped through the doorway then, a tall man, hands down by his sides, coat brushed back, bone handles jutting free . . .

He saw the Colonel standing by the back wall, just to one side of Sadie. Jerdney Smith was by the end of the long bar. Brawley was hanging back, close to the back door. Both men had guns in their hands.

They wouldn't shoot. Not yet. Not until they found out about the money.

The Colonel stepped away from the wall and moved toward Ryatt. His hands were empty, his tunic unbuttoned, his shoulder gun showing.

"You know where the money is, Luke?"

Luke nodded.

"Coster tell you?"

"No."

The Colonel didn't believe him.

"Coster didn't know where it was," Ryatt said. "Neither did Jeff." His voice was even, sure of itself. "That's why Jeff came in here that night. He thought you or one of your men had found it."

"That's why Morry Teague went out to the farm this morning," Ryatt said. "He didn't know where the money was. Like everyone else he thought it was buried somewhere on the farm —"

Brawley took a step forward, his eyes blazing. "Hell with it, Colonel! He's stalling —"

Behind the Colonel Sadie stirred . . . her eyes found Ryatt, widened, hope flickering . . .

"Luke . . . oh, Luke . . ."

"I'll make a deal with you," the Colonel said. "Four-way split. You walk out of here alive, with —" he looked back at Sadie, his voice thin with contempt, "with her and a quarter share of the money."

"No deal."

The Colonel's eyes flared. "You're a

Texan," he said bitterly. "Like us. You know Morry Teague robbed us. You don't owe this town anything."

"You killed Ned Coster," Ryatt said coldly. "Rafe told me —"

Jerdney broke first.

"Hell with the money!" he snarled, and brought his gun up, thumbing back on the spiked hammer.

Ryatt's hands jerked and came up, both guns blasting. Jerdney shuddered, staggered along the bar and fell . . .

Brawley, backing toward the door, fired hastily. Ryatt's slugs hammered him, knocked him back . . . he died with a curse on his lips.

The Colonel managed to get his shoulder gun out . . . managed to get it leveled . . . then his face exploded into a bloody mask just as he got a shot off.

Ryatt jammed his guns back into their holsters, made his way through the thickening smoke to Sadie and cut her loose.

She clung to him, crying.

He picked her up in his arms, feeling a twinge in his side, the bleeding starting again. He carried her outside.

Flames were roaring through the Lady Gay's upper floor as Ryatt went up the street to the Dodge House. He walked past staring, silent townspeople — a tall, grim-faced man with a naked, sobbing whore in his arms.

Only Angus MacIntosh came to help.

★ ★ ★

The morning sun slanted in against the window curtains of Ryatt's bedroom and fell across the bed.

Sadie stirred, opening her eyes. The nightmare was still with her. She cried out and sat up, the covers falling away from her. Her gaze searched the room.

"Luke! Oh, Luke . . ."

She sprang out of bed, ran to the window, and looked out. She craned her neck to see down the alley toward the street . . .

The door opened.

She whirled, a glad cry escaping from her. "Luke — thank God you haven't gone!"

She ran to him and threw her arms around his neck. "I thought you —"

"Easy," he said, smiling. "You'll spill the coffee."

He was carrying a tray with coffee, cups, biscuits, and her favorite jam.

"No champagne," he said. "Guess this will have to do."

She looked at him, tears coming.

"Come on now," he chided gently, "get back in bed."

She thought she understood what he meant . . . she obeyed. He set the tray down and tucked her in, pulling the coverlet up around her breasts. He brushed a tear from her cheek.

"Breakfast in bed," he said. His voice was

cheerful. He placed the tray down in front of her. "Coffee . . . biscuits . . . your favorite raspberry jam."

She didn't understand. No one had ever treated her like this before.

Luke reached inside his coat, took out a wallet, and counted out a number of gold-backed bills.

"Five thousand," he said, dropping the money down on the tray. "Should take care of you for a while, anyway."

She looked at the money.

"They paid me," Ryatt said. "The town fathers." He grinned. "I think they're glad to be rid of me."

"You're leaving?"

He nodded. "Job's finished."

"Take me with you?"

He shook his head.

"Will I see you again?"

"Sure," he said. "Sometime . . ."

He picked up his Boston bag, already packed, and checked his tie in the dresser mirror and the setting of his hat. His face looked a little drawn, but what the hell . . .

He bent over her and kissed her lightly on the mouth.

"Goodbye, Sadie."

The train for St. Louis was getting ready to leave. Ryatt walked into the station, bought a ticket, and went out to the platform. Passengers were already boarding. The conductor eyed him as Ryatt stepped up into the coach and headed back to the sleeping cars.

Amy Corby was seated by the window, looking out. She looked serenely happy in her widow's weeds.

He settled down beside her.

"Nice day," he commented.

She frosted him with a look. "Marshal —"

"Ex-marshal," he corrected her. He smiled. "The name's Luke Ryatt, just a plain ordinary citizen."

She turned her face away from him. The car jerked as couplings clashed . . . the train started to roll. Slowly Dodge City began to recede . . .

"I hope you're not going far," Amy said. Her tone was still icy.

He shrugged. "Only as far as you are."

Her head came around, lips compressed. There was an odd primness about her in that moment, a flash of self-righteousness.

"I thought you'd be staying behind," she said, "with that cheap little whore . . ."

"Needed a change," he said.

He took a cigar from his breast pocket. The bandages were still bulky around his middle, but the bleeding had stopped. And, like the good doctor had counseled, all he needed was a little bedrest.

"Where are you sleeping, Mrs. Corby?"

Her eyes widened. *"Mister Ryatt!"*

"Figure you'd like company," he said casually. He lighted up his cigar and puffed contentedly for a moment. "It's a long ride to St. Louis, and you need someone to help you spend Morry Teague's money."

She stared at him.

"You saw Jeff and Ned Coster hide it. You dug it up and hid it somewhere else . . ."

She smiled sweetly. "A likely story . . ."

He shrugged. "Shall we check through your bags, Mrs. Corby?"

She stiffened. "You wouldn't dare!"

He eased back against the seat.

She studied him for a long moment, then her eyes softened. She ran the tip of her tongue across her moist lips. She reminded him of Sadie . . . of all the women he had known.

"The name's Amy," she purred. She pointed. "First one down the aisle, on the left . . ."

Ryatt puffed on his cigar.

Yeah — it looked like it was going to be a pleasant trip to St. Louis.